"There are kisses— and there are kisses."

"Well," replied Christi, "maybe you could show me how they're done? I realize you would have to pretend to find me attractive, but at least then I'll know what to look for in a man," she concluded innocently.

"I don't think," he said darkly, "that would be a good idea."

"Then maybe I'll ask Barry. He goes out with starlets, and he should know—"

She was abruptly silenced when Lucas's mouth descended angrily on hers. In time the kiss changed. It became gentler, deeper, filled with passion. Christi was floating, soaring, feeling more complete than she ever had before.

Suddenly he thrust her away. Christi ran from his apartment with a choked sob. She'd seen the look of disgust on his face....

CAROLE MORTIMER, one of our most popular—and prolific—English authors, began writing in the Harlequin Presents series in 1979. She now has more than forty top-selling romances to her credit and shows no signs whatever of running out of plot ideas. She writes strong traditional romances with a distinctly modern appeal, and her winning way with characters and romantic plot twists has earned her an enthusiastic audience worldwide.

Books by Carole Mortimer

HARLEQUIN PRESENTS

HARLEQUIN SIGNATURE EDITION

CAROLE MORTIMER

to love again

Harlequin Books

TORONTO • NEW YORK • LONDON
AMSTERDAM • PARIS • SYDNEY • HAMBURG
STOCKHOLM • ATHENS • TOKYO • MILAN

Our sons,
Matthew and Joshua

Harlequin Presents first edition December 1988
ISBN 0-373-11131-2

Original hardcover edition published in 1988
by Mills & Boon Limited

CHAPTER ONE

CHRISTI stared in horror at the man who took up most of the open doorway to her flat, holding her hands up defensively. 'Whatever you do, don't come in here!' she warned fiercely.

To her chagrin he smiled, although he made no effort to come further into the room. 'What are you doing on the floor?' he drawled unconcernedly.

Christi came up off her hands and leant back on her knees. 'I—oh, no!' she groaned as a brown and grey bullet entered the room, finding herself almost knocked over as the tiny creature leapt up and down in front of her face, trying to lick her nose. 'No, Henry.' She desperately tried to still the movements of her excited Yorkshire terrier. 'Henry—— Oh, damn!' She gave in with a resigned groan, taking the dog into her arms to receive the ecstatic greeting.

'He's missed you.' Lucas made the understatement mockingly, grinning his amusement as Christi gave him a censorious frown.

'I've only been gone a couple of days,' she dismissed distractedly, her attention once again on the carpet in front of her now that Henry had calmed down enough to sit relatively still in her arms. 'Take him, will you?' She reached out to hold the dog up to Lucas. 'But don't come any closer,' she warned as Lucas strode forcefully into the room, having let himself into the apartment with the key she had given him.

He gave a weary sigh, coming to an abrupt halt. 'Make up your mind, Christi,' he said drily. 'Either I can come in, or I can't. Is there a man in your bedroom? Is that it?' He quirked dark brows interestedly.

Christi shot him a look that clearly told him the question was beneath contempt. 'I happen to have lost a contact lens——'

'Not again,' Lucas groaned impatiently. 'Last time you lost one of them it was down your——'

'I know where it was,' she put in hastily, blushing.

'Well, have you looked down there this time?' He looked speculatively at the creamy perfection of her cleavage, which was visible above the open neckline of her blouse. 'I could always help you if you haven't,' he flirted easily.

That was the trouble with Lucas; he flirted with lazy ease, having a constant stream of women in his life, who seemed to remain his friend even after the relationship had ended. He and Christi seemed to have skipped the first part and gone straight on to the friendship, Lucas's teasing of her just that. It was rather depressing to be thought of as just a 'pal' by a man like Lucas!

Everyone she had ever introduced him to had envied the fact that she actually had him living in the flat next door to her own. And that wasn't so surprising, for Lucas was devastating to look at; tall and dark, with piercing grey eyes that could be dark with laughter or glittering silver with anger, his body of the type that looked beautifully elegant in the superbly tailored suits he wore, or obviously masculine in the shorts he wore when he played tennis. He possessed a sense of humour that enchanted, a honeyed charm that enthralled, and a raw sexuality that acted like a magnet to any woman in the vicinity.

But he was also thirty-seven to her almost twenty-two, and had taken her under his protective wing since she had moved into this flat almost four years ago, acting more like her uncle than her real uncle did! He had also helped her find her missing contact lenses more times than she cared to think about, had taken care of her pets when she'd been away, and had fed her lemon juice when she had been flat out in bed with a cold, doing a good impersonation of Rudolf! No wonder he had never looked on her as anything more than 'the kid next door'—she *was* the kid next door!

'Just take Henry, will you?' She sighed her irritation. 'I haven't had the best of weekends, and if I can't find my lens I won't be able to go for that audition this afternoon.'

Lucas held the dog lightly in his arms as Christi resumed her search, her two Siamese cats entwining themselves about his long legs. He reached down to absently stroke Josephine and Gladys, straightening as Christi gave a triumphant cry, holding the truant lens as she scrambled to her feet to put it in before it did another disappearing act.

He frowned as she turned to face him. 'I thought you were looking forward to spending the weekend with Dizzy and your uncle.' He spoke slowly. 'There's nothing wrong with the baby, is there?' he added, concern in his voice.

Christi's expression instantly softened. 'Laura is the most beautiful, contented——'

'The baby is fine,' Lucas drawled drily.

'—little love I have ever seen,' Christi finished proudly. 'She has lovely golden curls—which is only to be expected when Dizzy and Uncle Zach—just Zach,' she amended with a grimace. 'He finally got around to telling me I can call him that, now that he's been married to my best friend for almost a year,' she derided. 'But, with both of them being so fair, Laura was sure to be blonde herself,' she completed her earlier statement.

Lucas looked pointedly at her ebony hair. 'They can't all be blondes in your family.'

'The Bennetts are,' she nodded. 'You know I got my colouring from my mother.' She experienced the usual sadness she felt whenever she thought of the wonderful parents she had lost four years ago, the two of them on an archaeological dig when it had capsized and buried them beneath tons of earth.

She hadn't been quite eighteen at the time, and remembered that the birthday she had spent with her Uncle Zach had been a miserable time, both of them numbed by the accident that had left them the only two remaining members of their family. Her uncle had been distant from her then, a remote professor of history who seemed to live among his books. Falling in love with impetuous madcap

Dizzy had changed all that, and when he wasn't amused by his young wife's antics he was *bemused*!

But, four years ago, Dizzy had been a long way from entering his life, and the two of them had found little to say to each other to ease the pain of their loss. Lucas had helped to ease her pain more than her uncle had, had held her as she'd cried bitter tears, had sat with her as she'd brooded in silence, had taken her out on picnics and walks when it seemed she would finally come out of the dark tunnel of depression her parents' deaths had caused.

Their friendship had grown from those months of anger and pain shortly after she had moved in here; it was a friendship Christi knew she would find it hard to live without now, and she dreaded the day one of those women in his life became more than lover and then friend, sure that another woman wouldn't welcome Lucas's friendship with her into their married life.

She wasn't conceited; as an actress she had been taught to evaluate her looks, to know her advantages and her limitations, and shoulder-length ebony hair, enormous sparkling blue eyes, straight nose, and widely curving mouth, tall and curving body, added up to quite a few advantages. No other woman was ever going to believe there was just friendship between herself and Lucas! She wasn't sure she believed it herself, considering how sexually attractive he was, having had more than her own share of men in her life. But friends they were, and it was a relationship they were both comfortable with. Certainly neither of them was willing to risk what they had for what would probably amount to a few days or weeks of being lovers.

'So what was wrong with your weekend?'

She frowned, concentrating with effort, her frown turning to a scowl as she thought over Lucas's question. 'Dizzy,' she began in a barely controlled voice, 'in her role as aunt and new mother, has decided that it's time I settled down myself——'

'*What?*' Lucas said incredulously.

'Oh, yes,' Christi confirmed disgustedly. 'Last year, Dizzy and Zach were worried because I didn't go out with anyone for more than a month, and *now* they're worried because I haven't seen anyone for six months!' She shook her head.

'Hm, I wondered about that myself——'

'Don't you start,' she warned, moving automatically to the kitchen to get her pets some breakfast as they all milled about her legs, Lucas having put Henry down long ago. 'I've been concentrating on my career the last six months,' she firmly informed Lucas as he came to lounge in the kitchen doorway.

He nodded. 'Nevertheless, it's been pretty quiet around here lately,' he mocked.

Christi gave him a look that clearly told him she didn't appreciate his humour. 'It's a pity the same can't be said for next door,' she returned waspishly, referring to the party he had held on the eve of her departure to the Lake District to visit her uncle and Dizzy.

'Ouch!' His eyes laughed at her. 'I did ask you to join us,' he reminded, not in the least perturbed by her complaint, knowing it wasn't justified, for his parties were never of the 'loud' variety.

Her bad humour faded as quickly as it had come; she hadn't really been angry. People who really knew her, and Lucas was one of them, knew that she was slow to anger. But when she did lose her temper it was best to take cover as soon as possible!

'It sounded like fun,' she conceded ruefully. 'But I had an early start Friday morning and I didn't want to be overtired.' She gave a heavy sigh. 'I wish now that I'd never gone! Oh, it was lovely seeing Laura for the first time, and I'm always pleased to spend time with Dizzy and Zach——'

'But?' Lucas prompted softly, taking out the cups to pour them both a cup of coffee from the pot, with the ease of familiarity.

'Thanks,' Christi accepted absently. She drew in a deep breath. 'But,' she sighed again, 'Dizzy had invited three of what she called "eligible" men for the weekend, too, for me to look over!' she concluded disgustedly.

Lucas just stared at her, his coffee-cup held unwaveringly in one slenderly masculine hand; for once, the articulate businessman, who could make a success of any company he chose to take over, was completely struck dumb.

Christi couldn't blame him; she had been more than a little speechless herself when Dizzy had calmly introduced the three men as their other weekend guests!

If she had met those men under any other circumstances, she probably would have found each of them as interesting as Dizzy assured her they were, but as the only female guest among three attractive men it had been instantly obvious what Dizzy was up to. Much as she loved her best friend from childhood, she could cheerfully have strangled her when they had all sat down to lunch and she'd found her attention demanded by each man in turn. Dizzy's intent was about as subtle as a sledgehammer, and Christi had spent a very embarrassing three days trying to fend off three fascinatingly attractive men. Some would have said she was mad to even try. Most would have known she had failed miserably when she had returned from the traumatic weekend with separate dates to see each man again!

Dizzy had been completely unconcerned by Christi's embarrassed protests about what she was up to, reminding Christi of a conversation they had once had about Christi advertising in a magazine for her ideal partner, sure she had as much chance of finding him that way as she did with any of the men she had dated so far. It had been a light-hearted conversation, made completely in fun on Christi's side, but Dizzy had obviously taken it seriously. While her marriage to Zach, and his obvious disapproval of such a ridiculous idea as advertising in a magazine, had been a foregone conclusion, Dizzy had done the next best thing as far as she was concerned, picking three men out of her close acquaintance that she was sure Christi would like, inviting them all together for the weekend, and sitting back to watch the results. The result had been that, after months of not dating anyone, Christi now had three different men to see in the next week!

She grimaced as she saw Lucas was still staring at her. 'You can close your mouth now,' she taunted, feeling the first stirrings of amusement over a weekend which at best had been awkward, at worst downright uncomfortable!

He did so slowly, sitting on the side of one of the bar stools that sided her breakfast bar. 'Dizzy seemed like a sane woman the one and only time I met her, when she married your uncle.' He spoke dazedly.

Christi grinned. 'You saw her on a good day, on her best behaviour.'

He shook his head. 'Has no one ever told her that the custom of choosing a husband for a female relative went out of style years ago?'

Her smile widened. 'Something as trivial as that isn't likely to stop Dizzy once she makes her mind up to an idea,' she dismissed ruefully, having years of experience to base her claim upon.

Lucas whistled softly through his teeth. 'So, what are you going to do?'

Embarrassed colour darkened her magnolia cheeks. 'I'm seeing Dick on Tuesday, Barry on Thursday, and David on Saturday,' she revealed reluctantly.

His mouth twisted. 'That's certainly showing Dizzy that she can't push you around!'

'I was in an awkward position,' Christi defended. 'I'd like to have seen you come out of it any differently.'

'My dear Christi,' he drawled derisively, 'no one pressures me into going out with someone I'd rather not.'

Her irritation increased, for she knew full well that a man like Lucas, who had remained single since his divorce several years ago, wouldn't be forced into doing *anything* he didn't want to do. But he was different from her, had a way of getting what he wanted, and away from what he didn't want, without anyone challenging his right to do so. That arrogance seemed to be a part of his nature he, and other people, took for granted; she just didn't have the same determination.

'I actually liked Dick, Barry and David,' she told him defensively.

He pulled a face, perfectly relaxed now that he was over his first surprise. 'Dick, Barry, and David who?' he drawled.

'Dick Crosby—Dizzy's agent,' she supplied a little resentfully. 'I've met him before, of course, since Dizzy began working as a freelance illustrator. Barry is Barry Robbins, a friend of my uncle's from his university days, who apparently put his studies to use in directing films in Hollywood,' she added challengingly as Lucas looked unimpressed.

'I've heard of him,' Lucas nodded dismissively.

'Hm,' she acknowledged irritably; the tall, blond-haired director was handsome enough to have appeared in his films rather than remaining behind the camera.

'I think I met Dick Crosby, at least, at the wedding,' Lucas remarked thoughtfully.

'Possibly,' she dismissed. 'I believe Barry was unable to get here in time.'

Because it hadn't seemed suitable to take a man to her uncle and Dizzy's wedding that she probably wouldn't see again a couple of weeks later, she had asked Lucas if he would accompany her instead. She had been thrilled when he'd accepted, proud to have had such an attractive man as her partner for the day.

'Just think yourself lucky you weren't one of the men chosen by Dizzy as suitable for me,' she told him disgustedly.

Lucas's mouth quirked. 'I wasn't "chosen" by her because I'm not suitable as far as you're concerned.' He tapped her playfully on the nose. 'I'm far too old for you, even if I'm not quite old enough to be your father. I think I certainly qualify for the role of a much older brother,' he added drily.

'My uncle is fourteen years older than Dizzy,' she defended.

'And they're obviously deliriously happy together,' he nodded. 'It's always the ones who are happy who are trying to pair everyone else off,' he explained at Christi's questioning look. 'But it isn't very often these spring and autumn relationships work out.'

'I think of Zach and Dizzy more as early summer and late spring,' she protested. 'I do know they're the best thing that ever happened to each other,' she added indulgently, never having seen Dizzy quite so confident of herself, nor her uncle quite so light-hearted, as they had been since they had fallen in love with each other.

'You haven't told me who the third man is yet,' Lucas reminded softly.

Because she had been saving the best until last! 'David Kendrick,' she revealed a little triumphantly, knowing he *had* to be impressed by the last man. 'Zach's publisher.'

Dark brows rose appreciatively. 'I know him quite well,' he nodded slowly.

It didn't surprise her in the least that David and Lucas should know each other; in fact, she remembered them talking briefly at the wedding last year, David acting as Zach's best man. As businessmen, Lucas and David had a lot in common, both seeming to have the Midas touch, their interests diversified but, without exception, successful.

'I have to agree with Dizzy about him,' she said softly.

'Why not Barry Robbins?' Lucas shrugged. 'You said he's a film director, and you're an actress, so maybe he'll be able to help your career.'

Her mouth tightened. 'I don't believe it's done that way any more!'

Lucas looked at her frowningly, then his mouth twitched with amusement as her meaning became clear, and finally he grinned openly. 'I meant if you were his wife, of course,' he said innocently.

'Of course,' she said sharply. 'But isn't that leaping into the future just a little?' she derided. 'I only have one date with the man. I certainly don't need you matchmaking, too!'

'Sorry,' he grimaced. 'I must try and remember that big brothers are for protecting you from big bad wolves like those three.'

Christi sighed, not appreciating his humour at her expense at all. She didn't find *anything* about the situation funny. 'Enough about my weekend,' she dismissed briskly. 'How did yours go?' she asked interestedly.

His humour instantly faded, a brooding look in his silver-grey eyes. 'Marsha didn't bring the children over until Saturday morning,' he revealed bitterly. 'Claimed Daisy had a temperature the day before.'

Christi gave him a sympathetic grimace. Lucas and his ex-wife didn't get on, and after she had met the brittly shallow woman a couple of times it wasn't too difficult to understand why a man as warm and charming as Lucas should find his ex-wife's grasping and manipulative nature highly distasteful.

Oh, Marsha hadn't always been that way, he had assured Christi. In fact, the two of them had been quite happy together when they had first married and produced first Robin and then Daisy. But, with the progression of their marriage, so had Lucas's success increased, and also Marsha's wants and ambitions. For the sake of their children, Lucas had given Marsha everything she asked for; he could afford it, so why not? Their marriage seemed to have survived only by Lucas giving and Marsha taking during the years. Until the day Marsha realised she could go on taking without having to remain married to Lucas.

Lucas had skimmed over the rocky years of his marriage to Marsha, playing down the difficult parts, enthusing over what a joy the children had been to him and Marsha both. It had been Marsha who had told Christi, in her brittle way, just how 'hellish' she had considered her marriage to Lucas to be, initially completely misunderstanding the friendship that existed between Christi and Lucas, warning her sharply of the dull life she could expect to lead if she became seriously involved with Lucas. Marsha's life as Lucas's wife had sounded far from dull to Christi, and her words more the fretful complaints of a spoilt woman.

As far as Christi could tell, Lucas's real regret at the breakdown five years ago of his four-year marriage was that his children had been left in Marsha's care, that he was only able to have seven-year-old Robin and six-year-old Daisy on the weekends and holidays Marsha agreed to let him have them.

It didn't seem right to Christi that such a woman should have the care of Lucas's children but, as he himself admitted, he had never been able to criticise Marsha's ability to be a mother to their two children.

But that caring didn't extend to the inclusions of bothering herself unduly about the feelings of the man she had dismissed so easily from her life once his wealth made it possible for her to still live lavishly without the restrictions of a husband, and so she didn't hesitate to callously let him down when he was expecting to see the children, always having a perfectly valid excuse for doing so, of course, so that there should be no legal repercussions.

Christie's heart ached for how much Lucas missed having his children with him all the time, how each time he saw them they seemed to have grown up a little more, achieved new things he had no sharing in. It was only the fact that Robin and Daisy seemed so well adjusted to the situation that prevented him being more bitter about things than he was.

But by the sound of it Marsha had been up to her usual tricks this weekend, seeming to take a fiendish delight in upsetting Lucas's plans for spending time with his children. Christi felt like shaking the other woman but, knowing the beautiful redhead, she would only laugh at accusations that she was being cruel to Lucas. She had claimed he didn't have a heart to be hurt on the one occasion Christi had tentatively mentioned how upsetting it must be for him to be parted from his children in this way.

Needless to say, there was no love lost between her and the other woman, although none of that showed as she smiled at Lucas. 'How did Daisy seem over the weekend?' she prompted lightly.

His expression softened. 'They were both fine. Having the cats and dog about the place helped,'

he added soberly, unconsciously revealing the strain
of only being allowed to be a part-time parent.

'I'm glad.' Christi gave a bright smile. 'Did Daisy
lose her other front tooth? You said it was a bit
wobbly the last time she stayed.'

The harshness of his face was completely softened
with love for the two mischievous imps that looked
so much like him, with their thick dark hair and
silver-grey eyes. 'Lost it and started to grow the re-
placement,' he answered ruefully.

'And did Robin like the Transformer you sent
for his birthday?' she smiled.

Lucas's mouth tightened, his eyes a fierce silver.
'His mother decided it wasn't suitable for him and
exchanged it for something else,' he rasped.

Christi gave a pained frown, sure that the toy
had been perfectly suitable for Robin. She had gone
with Lucas to shop for the sturdy toy, Lucas having
taken care not to buy anything with guns, re-
specting, and agreeing with, Marsha's decision that
Robin had plenty of time before he needed to be
introduced to the violence in life. The Transformer
they had finally chosen did no more than change
from a robust truck into a robot. What possible
harm could Marsha have found in that? The obvious thing seemed to be that his father had bought
it for him. The other woman wasn't averse to taking
what she could from Lucas—the monthly allowance she received from him was enough to keep
most families for a year!—but she wasn't about to
let Lucas take the praise for anything. Christi didn't

know how Lucas managed to control the anger he must feel towards his ex-wife!

'I'm sure he liked what he had instead,' she bit out tautly.

'He didn't say,' Lucas said grimly, glancing at his wristwatch as he stood up. 'I have an appointment at ten, so I have to go now,' he told her lightly, bringing back the smiling Lucas with effort. 'Good luck with the audition this afternoon.' He nudged her gently under the chin with his fist. 'Break a leg,' he teased.

She returned his smile. 'Thanks for looking after the pets for me.' She walked him to the door.

'My pleasure.' He moved with leashed vitality, grinning at her as they reached the door. 'And I shall expect a full report on your dates this week,' he derided. 'And remember, as an honorary brother, I expect an invitation to the wedding,' came his parting shot.

Christi watched him stride off down the corridor to the lift, returning his brief salute before the doors closed behind him.

Oh, she would honour the dates she had made with the three men while they were in the Lake District, but she knew with certainty that a wedding wouldn't result from seeing any of them again.

How could she marry anyone when it was Lucas she loved, that she had always loved?

CHAPTER TWO

PERHAPS always was putting it a little strongly, but Christi had certainly loved Lucas from the time he had first introduced himself as her neighbour almost four years ago.

Her parents had only recently died, the full impact of that not hitting her until weeks later, and her move from her parents' house to a smaller, more manageable apartment had been made with something like detachment. Certainly, it hadn't been until some of the suitable furniture from her parents' home was being moved into the apartment that she suddenly realised her mother would never be coming back to sit behind the delicate writing-table as she answered all her overdue correspondence, that her father—her dear, absent-minded father—wouldn't ever again have a need for the display cabinet that had housed his most precious objects, those artefacts now given to museums, as he had requested they should be in his will.

But seeing all that furniture moved into these strange surroundings had been the end for her. She had run from the apartment with a choked cry, coming to an abrupt halt as she crashed into a hard, but somehow soft, wall. Lucas's chest . . .

She had been eighteen years old, sheltered and cosseted all her life by over-indulgent parents, the men she had so far had in her life only a passing amusement at best. But, as she looked up into the harshly beautiful face of the man that held her so tightly against his chest, she had felt her heart leave her body and join with his. Not even a word had passed between them, but Christi knew she was looking into the face of the man she loved.

And when he had spoken it had been with gentle kindness, introducing himself as Lucas Kingsley, her new neighbour, insisting she join him in his apartment for a drink of some kind while the removal men finished bringing up her furniture.

Christi had felt wrapped in a protective glow, huskily explaining her recent loss, held tightly in his arms as she cried on his broad shoulder, her senses wallowing in the clean smell of him that was mingled with another smell that was all Lucas, a completely masculine aura that seduced and tempted, drawing her more fully into his spell.

He had left her only briefly, and that was to tip the removal men when they knocked on the door to say they had finished, returning instantly to take her in his arms once again.

But, during that time, or the many times afterwards when he had offered her the same comfort, it had never been the sort of embrace she wanted from him. He treated her more like the little sister he had never had, taking her firmly under his wing until she felt able to stand on her own two shaky feet, even then continuing to be the shoulder she could always cry on if she felt the need.

She had watched with dismay as first one woman entered his life, and then another, none of them lasting very long, all of them maintaining a friendship even once the relationship was over. With each new woman that entered his life, Christi lived in dread of this one being the one he decided to settle down with.

After two years of loving him that hopelessly, when it seemed he would never see her as more than the 'little girl next door,' she had decided something would have to be done to make him see she was all grown up now, a woman in every sense of the word. If she couldn't have Lucas, she was going to make sure he saw her with enough men to be convinced of her maturity.

The next year had been full of those men, but, instead of Lucas accepting she was no longer a child, he had merely offered her his shoulder to cry on whenever one of those friendships broke up!

After more careful thought, she had decided that it had to be the fact that she still had a guardian, in the shape of her uncle Zach, that prevented Lucas seeing her maturity, and consequently her love for him. That decision had provoked an elaborate—and, she accepted now a ridiculous—plan, that would show her uncle just how adept she was at taking responsibility for her own life. The result of that had been her uncle and Dizzy—who she had somehow managed to persuade to enter into the madcap scheme to hoodwink her uncle—falling in love with each other, her uncle releasing his guardianship of her and her inheritance into her own control at twenty-one, instead of the twenty-five it could have been—and with Lucas's attitude not changing towards her in the least!

She had been at a loss to know *what* to do after that, had drifted along for another six months, lost in a sea of self-pity. Then, as a last desperate plea for Lucas's love, she had stopped dating other men altogether, concentrating on her career, hoping that would finally make him sit up and take notice of her. Months later, she had to admit it hadn't affected him in the slightest.

And neither had the idea of her possibly becoming involved with Dick Crosby, Barry Robbins, or David Kendrick! He had even invited himself to the wedding!

She would just have to accept it, she didn't have anything to interest a man of thirty-seven who had been married and had a couple of children.

She couldn't accept that! She loved Lucas, had loved him for four long years, would go on loving him until the day she died. And she wouldn't give up trying to get him to return that love until that day came!

The last thing she felt like doing at the end of another exhausting—and disappointing—day, was getting dressed up to go out on a date with Dick Crosby.

She freely admitted that she had got out of the habit of going out on dates the last six months. Not that it had been too difficult; until last week she had had a one-line part in a long-running play, which had taken up most of her evenings. But last week the play had come to an end, and so she was back looking for work, or 'resting', as most people knew it. She knew she was one of the lucky ones; her allowance, and then her full inheritance, meant that she was never going to be one of the 'starving' actors who had to find work to survive. But she wanted to make a success of her career, and loved to act, going for any of the auditions her agent managed to set up for her. It was a bit much to expect success after only two days of looking, but the fact that she hadn't didn't add to the mood of wanting to go out for the evening.

It didn't help that she hadn't seen Lucas since he had so blithely invited himself to her non-existent wedding, either!

He had been out on a date last night himself, with a beautiful lawyer who possessed brains as well as all that blonde beauty; Christi had learnt this when Lucas introduced the two of them last week. He and Michelle had been seeing each other for a couple of weeks now, and Christi could tell by the way Michelle looked at Lucas that she was more than fond of him. It was like twisting a knife in her chest to see him with other women, to imagine him making love to those women. One thing she was grateful for, Lucas never brought those women home to spend the night with him, any lovemaking he did obviously taking place at the woman's home.

He had come home alone last night, late, because Christi had heard him letting himself into his apartment just after twelve.

He had already left for the office in town, from which he ran his considerable empire, by the time she'd got up this morning; and as she wasn't likely to see him tonight, either, now that she was going out herself, the evening looked bleak.

Poor Dick Crosby! She wasn't being fair to him at all, she realised ruefully. He couldn't help it if he wasn't the man she really wanted to be with, nor that she was in love with a man who was far out of her reach.

Because she felt so guilty about her reluctance to go on this date at all, she made an extra special effort to look nice for Dick, aware that the flaming red dress, that reached just below her shapely knees, made her hair appear more ebony than usual, and added colour to her pale cheeks.

Nevertheless, her heart gave a weary lurch when the doorbell rang promptly at eight o'clock, and there was no way she could force a sparkle into haunted blue eyes as she hurried to answer the door.

Dick Crosby was in his early thirties, with thick sandy-coloured hair that fell endearingly across his forehead, and brown eyes that warmed appreciatively as they took in her appearance. Not quite six feet tall, he nevertheless possessed a natural grace of movement that made him appear taller than he actually was.

'I must remember to thank Dizzy for finally introducing us properly,' he murmured softly.

Dizzy. Her best friend—and aunt—had rung her shortly after she had got in this evening, assuring her what a lovely person Dick was, and telling her to 'give him a chance'.

Mentioning Dizzy was the worst thing Dick could have done, if he had but known it, the evening losing what little glow it had had with the remembrance that Dizzy had been the one to set them up in this way. She meant well, but ...

'Shall we go?' Christi suggested sharply, sighing inwardly as Dick gave her a hurt look. 'Sorry,' she grimaced. 'Bad day,' she excused, picking up her jacket to follow him out into the corridor.

He relaxed again. 'Oh, I know what they are,' he said knowingly. 'Only too well, lately.'

'Oh?' she prompted with polite interest. Maybe if she got him chatting she wouldn't have to add too much to the conversation.

'Yes, I——' Dick broke off abruptly as he saw the stricken look on her face as the lift doors opened in front of them.

Christi stared disbelievingly at Lucas and Marsha as they stood side by side in the lift. Lucas was grim-faced, Marsha as kittenishly beautiful as usual as her ex-husband ushered her out into the corridor.

The two couples stared at each other as the lift doors closed, and the lift descended again without Christi having made a move to go inside it.

Marsha and Lucas made an arresting couple— Lucas so tall and handsome, Marsha so delicately lovely as her hand rested on the crook of his arm.

But what were they doing together like this? the question screamed in Christi's mind. How could Lucas *fail* to appreciate the beauty of the woman

who had once been his wife, her hair curving
alluringly about her beautiful heart-shaped face,
the black dress she wore showing off her curves to
perfection. Next to her, Christi felt like an ungainly
giraffe!

And then reality righted itself, and with it came
the realisation that Lucas and Marsha were divorced because they didn't love each other, that they
had been more like enemies the last five years, that
the only interest they shared was their children.

The children... Of course! Marsha would be here
to discuss something with Lucas concerning the
children. She could only hope, for Lucas's sake,
that it was nothing too traumatic; Marsha had
already made him suffer enough where they were
concerned.

'You seem to have missed the lift,' Marsha purred
mockingly, hazel-coloured eyes gleaming with
catlike malice as she looked Christi over scornfully.

Christi's head went back challengingly. 'It must
be the surprise of seeing you again,' she derided.
'It must be—almost a year since we last met?'

'Something like that,' the other woman dismissed in a bored voice. 'You haven't changed at
all,' she scorned. 'Although the men in your life
seem to have matured somewhat.' She looked Dick
over appreciatively, giving him her most seductive
smile.

Christi stiffened at Marsha's open derision for
her lack of years, glancing uncomfortably at Lucas.
He looked so grim, his eyes glittering silver with
suppressed anger, that Christi just wanted to put

her arms around him and tell him everything would be all right, that Marsha wouldn't be able to torment him with the upbringing of his children any longer. But it would be a hollow promise; while Marsha had Lucas's children, she took great delight in making him dance to her tune any time she wished. For a man as forceful and dynamic as Lucas, it was an impossible situation.

She woodenly made the introductions. Lucas's greeting was terse, to say the least, Marsha's a sensuous purr, and Dick's after his initial surprise at hearing that Marsha and Lucas, the flirtatious woman and the grim-faced man, were husband and wife, was cautiously warm; he kept a wary eye on the other man's face with its stony expression and hooded grey eyes. He obviously didn't know what to make of the oddly matched pair, and Christi took pity on him and suggested they had better leave now or they would be late for dinner.

She cast one last anxious glance at Lucas as the lift doors closed behind her and Dick, her heart twisting at how bleak he looked.

'What a strange couple,' Dick remarked dazedly at her side.

Christi's mouth tightened. 'They're divorced,' she snapped.

'Oh!' he said with some relief. 'Oh,' he repeated again in soft speculation.

'And yes, Marsha is very available, in case you're interested,' she told him sharply, marching out of the building to come to a halt on the edge of the pavement. She was shaking with anger, and drew in a deep, steadying breath to calm herself.

Dick caught up with her in a couple of strides; he seemed surprised by her outburst, and looked at her enquiringly.

'I'm sorry.' She gave a rueful grimace. 'Marsha doesn't bring out the best in me, and—well, I did warn you it had been a bad day.' And it was getting worse by the moment! Dick couldn't be blamed for finding Marsha attractive, especially after the woman had come on to him as strongly as she had. At the time, it had just seemed to her that Marsha was to blame for the fact that Lucas wasn't able to fall in love again, and that the man Christi did have interested in her was also succumbing to the other woman's undoubted sensual attraction. In that moment, it had just seemed too much! 'Although that's no reason to behave like a shrew,' she apologised again.

This time, instead of feeling annoyance when Dick mentioned Dizzy, Christi felt relieved to be on neutral ground, relaxing slowly on the drive to the restaurant as they discussed the success of Dizzy's illustrations. The most recent publication to come out with one of her illustrations was a Claudia Laurence book, one of the most successful ever.

Not many people realised it, but Christi's uncle Zach was, in fact, Claudia Laurence, the author of those 'hot' historicals that always had the public clamouring for more. Christi herself had found out quite by accident, shocked to learn that the man she had once termed 'fusty and dusty' wrote those enjoyable adventurous romps. As Dizzy's agent, Dick was also in on the secret, and they both relaxed as they discussed the books.

Her uncle's secret was one she hadn't even told Lucas, knowing how sensitive her uncle was about the subject, for his career as a professor of history was just as important to him. It wasn't that she thought Lucas would tell anyone else, it was just that—well, it wasn't her secret to tell. Maybe if he had been able to love her...

'Is there anyone there?' Dick spoke in a ghostly voice.

Christi blinked at him in surprise, having been completely unaware of her surroundings; the exclusive restaurant, and Dick, had faded from her mind as her thoughts had once again dwelled on Lucas.

'I'm so sorry,' she apologised again. 'I'm afraid I'm not very good company tonight,' she added with embarrassment.

'That's all right,' he accepted ruefully. 'I guess my conversation must have been boring for you.'

She had no idea what the conversation had been about! But Dick didn't seem about to go over it again, suggesting they order their meal instead.

Christi felt terrible about her inattentiveness, putting Lucas—and what Marsha could possibly want to see him about—firmly from her mind, and concentrating on being charming to Dick.

Nevertheless, it wasn't the most successful evening she had ever had, and as Dick kissed her briefly at her door, obviously waiting for an invitation to come in, she knew it would be kinder not to encourage him any further. He was a nice enough man, but he certainly wasn't going to be the one to supplant Lucas in her heart!

'No?' he realised gently.

Christi gave a shaky smile. 'I am sorry——' She was silenced by his fingertips over her lips.

'It was a nice evening,' he smiled. 'I enjoyed your company—I'm not so sure you were actually with me most of the evening,' he teased without rancour, 'but it was a pleasant time.'

Pleasant. It wasn't much of a eulogy. She had to face it: as a return to the dating scene, it had been a disaster!

She was shaking her head as she walked aimlessly around her apartment, filled with a restlessness that wouldn't be satisfied until she had spoken to Lucas again. But she couldn't go knocking on his door at eleven-thirty at night!

Damn it, *why* couldn't she? They were friends, at least, and friends cared about each other, and he had looked awful when she saw him earlier with Marsha. He could even be ill. Or...

Why bother to search for excuses? She *had* to talk to him, and that was all there was to it!

Christi was encouraged by the fact that she could hear music playing softly inside the apartment next to hers, and hesitated only briefly outside the door as the possibility that he wasn't alone passed through her mind. She would take that risk; he could only ask her to wait until tomorrow before talking to him.

She knew she had been right to come when she saw how haggard he looked when he opened the door to her ring, his dark hair looking as if he had been running agitated fingers through it for most of the evening, his face pale, his pale grey shirt partly unbuttoned down his chest to reveal the start of the dark hair that grew there, a glass of whisky held in his hand. It was the latter that told her how disturbed he was; Lucas never drank alcohol, and only ever kept a supply in for guests.

She shifted uncomfortably on his doorstep as he looked at her with narrowed eyes. 'I—er—I thought I would come and tell you how my evening went.' It was positively the last thing she had meant to say, but suddenly she had felt as if she were intruding on something he didn't want to talk about just now. 'You did say you would like a report on each of my dates,' she added lamely as he continued to look at her.

To her relief, he relaxed slightly, a faint glimmer of amusement darkening his eyes as he held the door wider for her to enter.

The lounge was in shadows, with only a small table-lamp for illumination, the Kenny Rogers cassette she had bought him last Christmas playing softly in the background. Christi turned awkwardly to face Lucas, feeling as if she had walked in on something very private. What *had* Marsha wanted to talk to him about tonight?

'No Michelle tonight?' she enquired lightly as she sat down in one of the comfortable brown leather armchairs, the room completely masculine, the décor brown and cream, the furniture heavy and attractive.

'No,' he drawled, his voice gruff, as if the unaccustomed raw alcohol had burned his throat on its way down. 'I didn't think it fair to inflict my company on anyone tonight,' he added ruefully, taking another drink of the whisky as he dropped down on to the sofa, his long legs stretched out in front of him.

Maybe she should have had the same forethought, and not ruined Dick Crosby's evening for him! Dizzy was sure to telephone for a full report tomorrow, and she wasn't going to be too happy with what she was told.

Strange, she and Dizzy were closer than sisters, and yet she had never told her friend of her love for Lucas, had never told anyone. God knew *what* Dizzy would do if she knew it was Lucas she loved! Christi thought disgustedly.

But, right now, dealing with Lucas's depressed mood, a mood she had never seen him in before in all the years she had known him, was what was important to her. Lucas's happiness would always be important to her.

'So,' he spoke briskly, 'was he the one?' He looked at her interestedly, amusement darkening his eyes.

Christi relaxed slightly at his teasing. 'No,' she answered without hesitation.

'Oh!' Lucas looked surprised. 'He seemed a nice enough chap to me.'

'He was,' she nodded. 'But he wasn't for me.' You're the man for me, she cried inside, wishing— oh, God, *wishing* he could see her as more than a young sister, or, even worse, someone he treated as being on the same age level as his two children! Much as she liked Robin and Daisy, her feelings towards them weren't sibling, but more maternal. She longed to be their stepmother, to perhaps give Lucas other children. 'Crying for the moon,' her mother would probably have told her gently, her face softened with love.

Lucas sipped his whisky again. 'How could you tell after just one date? Love doesn't always hit you between the eyes like a fist, you know. Sometimes it takes time to develop and grow.' He relaxed back against the sofa, watching her beneath heavy lids.

But sometimes it did hit you like that fist, and when it did it was the hardest thing in the world to live without! 'Love doesn't,' she acknowledged with a nod.

He frowned. 'Meaning something else does?'

'Oh, yes,' she smiled.

'What—ah!' He gave a knowing sigh, his mouth twisted into a smile. 'That little monster lust rearing its head again,' he derided.

The bleakness was starting to fade from his eyes, and he had put down the half-finished glass of whisky on the coffee-table beside him. 'I don't think of it as lust,' she chided reprovingly. 'Merely a case of physical attraction,' she corrected with mock indignation, rewarded with a gleam of laughter in dark grey eyes.

'Lust,' he repeated drily. 'But there was none of this—physical attraction,' he teased her mockingly, 'between you and Dick Crosby?'

Another few moments of this nonsense and she would have the old Lucas back again, and not the man whose barely leashed savagery distressed her so much.

'Hm—maybe a little,' she conceded with exaggerated thought.

'On his part, at least,' Lucas taunted knowingly. 'Weren't you attracted to him, too?' he asked interestedly.

'He was very handsome, fun to be with,' she conceded with a shrug.

'And?'

'And nothing,' she dismissed lightly.

'You liked him, he was fun to be with, you found him handsome, and yet—nothing?' Lucas said disbelievingly.

'Hm,' she nodded, mischief gleaming in her eyes. 'I had my doubts throughout the evening, but it was the kiss that finally convinced me,' she said sadly, laughter lighting up her eyes beneath demurely lowered lashes.

Lucas sat forward, his elbows resting on his knees, a frown between his eyes. 'The man has got to the age of—thirty-one, thirty-two——'

'Thirty-one,' she confirmed.

'To the age of thirty-one, and is still a lousy kisser?' he said incredulously.

'On the contrary,' she drawled, 'he was a very experienced and accomplished kisser.'

'But——'

'There are kisses. And then there are kisses, Lucas,' she explained meaningfully, knowing they wouldn't be having this conversation at all if Lucas hadn't drunk the unaccustomed whisky. In the past, he had always shown a cursory interest in her dates, but they had certainly never discussed these sort of intimacies!

'There are?' he mocked.

'Platonic kisses, polite kisses, meaningless kisses——'

'I thought there was only *one* way for a man to kiss a woman he found attractive,' Lucas drawled. 'So that he leaves her in no doubt that he wants her.'

Christi felt her heart leap in her chest, knowing she could lose what she already had with Lucas, but also knowing she would perhaps never have another opportunity like this one. 'Then maybe Dick did do something wrong,' she accepted thoughtfully. 'Maybe you could show me how it should be done? Oh, I realise you would have to pretend to find me attractive, but at least this way I know what to look for in a man,' she concluded innocently, her hands clasped tightly together so that Lucas shouldn't see their trembling, her heart beating so loudly, she felt sure he must be able to hear it. She *could* lose everything with him, but oh, how she longed to know the touch of his lips on hers just once!

His expression darkened. 'I don't think——'

She quickly got up from her chair and joined him on the sofa, her legs folded beneath her as she faced him. 'How else am I to know what to want from a man if someone doesn't show me?' She looked at him imploringly.

He swallowed hard, a nerve pulsing at his jaw. 'The men you dated last year——'

'Did nothing for me, either,' she dismissed, telling him clearly that she had never found any man attractive enough to let him do more than kiss her.

How could she let any other man but Lucas touch her? She had loved him long before she had taken any other man seriously, and loving Lucas as she did meant she couldn't bear the thought of any other man making love to her.

Her heart pounded more loudly than ever as she waited for his answer, knowing she was perhaps taking advantage of the fogging the whisky had caused to his brain, but wanting—*so much*—to be taken in his arms. Regrets could come later. And she didn't doubt that there would be many.

Lucas sighed, shaking his head, obviously not as affected by the whisky as she had thought—hoped!—he was. 'I don't think that would be a good idea.'

She sat back with a shaky sigh, his rejection a bitter blow. 'Maybe Barry will be more co-operative,' she challenged angrily, blinking back her tears of disappointment. 'After mixing with all those Hollywood starlets, he's sure to be very experienced!'

Lucas clasped her arms, turning her to face him, his expression fierce. 'Don't go playing games with a man like Barry Robbins,' he warned grimly.

'Why not?' she said defiantly, so hurt she just had to hit out at him. She had taken the chance, and lost, but in a way that humiliated as much as it hurt. 'He's attracted to me, I can tell, and— oomph!' She was abruptly silenced as Lucas's mouth descended on hers, stealing her breath away.

He was kissing her out of anger, not passion, but to Christi it didn't matter; she melted into his arms as he bent her back against the sofa, her arms moving up about his neck as she clung to him, gladly returning his kiss.

And then his mouth gentled on hers, controlling the fiery passion that had instantly blazed between them, nibbling on her lips with slow enjoyment, tracing the outline of lips with the tip of his tongue, moving it temptingly against them, but making no attempt to probe within, promising but not giving.

Christi's body ached, her nipples hard pebbles against his chest as the kiss once again became fierce, no longer promising but giving fully, plunging again and again until her whole body shook and quivered with need, a need which was slightly assuaged when his hands began to move restlessly over her aching flesh.

She was floating, she was soaring, she was held totally captive, she was aching, she was hurting, she was more complete than she had ever felt before. She was Lucas's . . .

Suddenly he thrust her away from him, staring down at her as if he couldn't believe his eyes, moving forcefully up off the sofa to move as far away from her as possible, his back rigidly unyielding as he kept himself firmly turned away from her.

Christi knew how she must look to him, her eyes drugged with wantonness, her mouth a swollen pout, her hair wild about her shoulders, her breasts still thrusting against the soft material of her dress, that same dress having ridden up to show off the long expanse of her thighs.

And the wanton Lucas had produced obviously disgusted him.

She got up from the sofa with a choked sob, running from the room, from the apartment. She didn't stop running until she was safely hidden away in her bedroom.

CHAPTER THREE

IF CHRISTI had expected Lucas to follow her, to try to make things right between them again, she had been disappointed. He didn't come to her that night, and she saw nothing of him the next day, either, whether by his design or by coincidence she didn't know. She did know that he wasn't at his apartment all day and that he didn't even return to change before going out for the evening, although she had heard his return at three o'clock this morning.

She had ruined things between them, had pushed their friendship through a barrier Lucas had no wish for it to cross.

She curled up into an even tighter ball of misery as she lay in her bed at nine o'clock in the morning, trying to force herself to get out and get herself moving.

She had wanted Lucas as a lover, yes, but she didn't have that, and she certainly didn't have his friendship any more, either. At the time, she had wanted him so badly it hadn't seemed to matter, but after just one day of knowing she disgusted him she was finding it hard to live with herself.

What if she never saw him again? What if he decided to move out of his apartment because of the uncomfortable situation she had forced upon

44

them? Until these last two days, it had never occurred to her that Lucas would ever move away from living next door to her. But she had to admit that now it was more than a possibility. She tried to tell herself that she was too good a friend to Lucas for this upset to cause him to do that, but at the same time she knew she had made it impossible for him to feel comfortable in his own home.

Then she would have to be the one to move out! Why should Lucas be forced out for something that had all been her fault, because her curiosity and good sense had got the better of her?

She didn't want to move, hated the thought of moving away from here, from possibly never seeing Lucas again. But if one of them had to go it would have to be her; she had no choice.

That decision made, she got wearily out of bed, the day stretching in front of her. She had no auditions to go to, no one to see until Barry Robbins tonight. 'Resting' was all well and good, but it gave you too much time to think and brood. About what might have been. How different things might have been if Lucas had known the same passion and desire she had the other night, she mused dreamily. They would have made love together all night, spent the day together, probably been together again last night, too. Instead of that, they weren't even talking to each other.

Whoever would have thought she and Lucas would come to this? What had possessed *her* to force that situation of the other night?

Tears that had fallen all too readily over the last two days began to roll down her cheeks again. Oh, Lucas! she cried inside as she dropped down on one of the bar stools in her kitchen, the homely sound of the coffee percolating not piercing her misery. How often she and Lucas had sat down and had coffee together before he left to go to work, and how she had daydreamed, during those times, that they were a happily married couple sharing breakfast together. Reality had intruded when Lucas had stood up to kiss her paternally on the forehead, or, worse than that, had ruffled her hair affectionately before picking up his briefcase and leaving.

Christi gave a startled jump as her doorbell rang, hastily brushing away her tears as she went to greet the doorman with her mail.

But it was Lucas who stood on the doorstep, and she gazed up at him apprehensively. Not that she was in the least self-conscious about having him see her in her short pink silk nightshirt; she had breakfasted with him hundreds of times in the past wearing similar night attire. It was having him treat her as a stranger that was going to be so unbearable.

'Good morning, lazybones,' he greeted with an indulgent grin, ruffling her hair affectionately as he strode inside her apartment.

Christi followed him dazedly after closing the door behind him; this was no stranger, this was the Lucas she had always known!

'I was in my apartment working when I heard you moving about—at last!' he rebuked teasingly,

grey eyes dark with affection. 'I knew you would
be putting coffee on, so I thought I'd come over
and share a cup with you.' He strode into the
kitchen with the ease of familiarity, getting down
the cups for their coffee. 'I must say, you look a
little hung-over this morning, Christi.' He handed
her a cup of steaming coffee.

She looked hung-over? *He* was the one who had
come home at three o'clock this morning! Not that
he looked any the worse for it; he was exuding good
health and vitality, while she—— Obviously what
had happened between them the other evening certainly hadn't kept *him* awake at nights!

Instead of feeling guilty about what had happened, Christi began to feel anger at Lucas's in-
difference. Didn't the passion they had shared mean
anything to him? Obviously not, she decided
indignantly.

Unless he just didn't remember it? He had been
drinking that evening, something he rarely did, and
maybe, just maybe—— But wasn't that the classic
excuse people used when something had happened
they would rather just forget, and didn't know how
else to achieve it?

She looked at Lucas suspiciously. Was that why
he was behaving like his usual cheerful self this
morning, because he wanted her to *think* he didn't
even remember what had happened between them
the other night, because he wanted to forget the
whole embarrassing incident *had* happened? Or—
and this seemed more like the Lucas she loved—
was he trying to save face for both of them, hoping

that, if he behaved as if nothing had happened between them, they would eventually both feel that nothing *had* happened?

Christi would give anything not to live through the mortification of the last two days again, and readily accepted that Lucas thought the whole thing was best forgotten, grasping at the friendship he offered with both hands.

At least, she took the coffee he held out to her with both hands, giving him a relieved smile!

He settled himself on one of her bar stools, facing out towards the kitchen, breathtakingly attractive in the dark navy suit and snowy white shirt, his striped tie meticulously knotted at his throat, his dark hair falling endearingly across his forehead.

'So,' he said lightly. 'Did you go out last night?' he asked interestedly.

'No.' She would have liked to ask him where he had been until three o'clock this morning but, considering Michelle's obvious beauty, and his continuing relationship with the other woman, the answer to that was all too obvious. And painful. 'I had a few chores to do,' she dismissed shruggingly. 'Did you have a pleasant evening?' She looked at him enquiringly.

'Fine,' he nodded. 'How are the auditions going?'

She gave a rueful smile. 'They aren't.' She sighed. 'There are too many actresses and not enough parts.'

'Hm, it's a pity the play had to close,' he nodded thoughtfully.

They were talking as they usually did, and yet to Christi there was something missing. At first, it was difficult to pinpoint, and then she knew it was the ease with which they were usually together. Unless it was just her, because Lucas seemed just as relaxed as ever. Maybe he really *didn't* remember the other night? Wouldn't he have mentioned it if he did remember, tried to clear the air?

She didn't know any more, all she did know was that Lucas was her friend again. She wasn't about to risk that friendship a second time, even if being kissed by him had been the most beautiful experience of her life!

'—something to offer you,' Lucas was saying as her thoughts came back to their conversation.

'Sorry?' She gave a grimace of apology for her inattentiveness.

He gave a rueful smile. 'I said, maybe Barry Robbins will have something he can offer you,' he suggested lightly.

Christi frowned. The other evening, Lucas had more or less warned her off the film director, now he seemed to find nothing wrong in again suggesting she use the man's connections to get herself work. But if he didn't remember what he had said the other night ... It was becoming more and more obvious that he really didn't.

Her mouth twisted. 'I'm not sure I'm the type of material for Hollywood,' she derided.

'You're certainly more beautiful than most of those so-called stars over there,' Lucas encouraged.

What was the good of being beautiful if that beauty didn't appeal to the one man she wanted it to? 'Thank you, kind sir!' She curtseyed in the above-knee-length nightshirt. 'I'll be sure to tell Barry you said so,' she teased, feeling more relaxed by the minute, knowing now wasn't the time to introduce the subject of Marsha's visit the other night, and rekindle the discord.

Lucas stood up, glancing at his watch. 'If the man can't see that for himself, then maybe he ought to give up film directing,' he taunted. 'I have an appointment in half an hour, so I have to go now. Have a good time this evening,' he called as he let himself out. 'I'll be in later if you want to come and tell me all about your date.'

Christi rushed into the hallway just as the door closed firmly behind him. What had he meant by *that*? Had it been the casual remark it had seemed— or something more?

God, her whole world seemed to have turned upside-down since Tuesday night, so that she didn't know her right from her left any more. She had thought she knew Lucas so well, now she wasn't sure she knew him at all.

If Dizzy had hoped to introduce her to the man she could fall in love with last weekend, all she had done was cause more confusion!

Barry Robbins was undoubtedly one of the most handsome men Christi had ever met; slightly overlong blond hair that curled attractively at his nape and ears, sexy blue eyes that left her in no doubt as to his appreciation of her own looks, a tall, lithe body that could look as good in the casual clothes he had worn last weekend as he did in the biscuit-coloured suit and pale cream shirt he wore tonight, the plain brown tie a perfect complement to the more flamboyant suit.

And Englishman by birth, his years in America had given him a slight, and wholly appealing, drawl to his accent, and Christi enjoyed just hearing him talk. Which was perhaps as well, when she couldn't find a lot to say herself!

Barry had arrived exactly on time, refusing to come in for a drink, taking her to dinner before going on to the stage musical she had been meaning to go and see for months but which she hadn't found the time to do when the play she was in was showing at the same times.

They went to a quiet bar after the show, the first few minutes taken up with discussing the merits of the performance. Usually vivacious, Christi found it heavy going after that; she couldn't help glancing at her watch, wondering if it would be too late to take Lucas up on his invitation if she left now.

'I thought you weren't working at the moment,' Barry finally remarked.

Christi blushed guiltily. 'I'm not. I—I'm just a bit of a clock-watcher,' she excused lamely. 'It comes from months of making sure I was always on time for a performance, I expect.' She gave a bright smile.

'Yes,' he chuckled knowingly. 'I know I come to startled wakefulness for weeks after I've finished making a film, wondering why no one has woken me up at the crack of dawn! The stringent time-keeping is part of the business,' he said understandingly.

Christi relaxed once again; the two of them had so much in common, after all. 'You aren't working at the moment?' she prompted interestedly.

'I start filming late next week,' he dismissed. 'But I'm working on another project at the moment.'

'Sounds mysterious,' she teased, sipping her wine, having decided she had better stick with the one drink all evening.

'Not really,' Barry smiled. 'You know this business as well as I do; one minute you have a feasible idea, the next it's back to the proverbial drawing-board.'

'Like the play I was in,' she acknowledged heavily.

Barry looked at her consideringly. 'With your looks, I'm sure you would do well in Hollywood.'

So much for having to tell this man Lucas's totally biased opinion, she thought moodily. She didn't want to go to Hollywood, away from everything she held dear, away from Lucas!

'Just say the word and I'll——'

'Thanks, but I'm really not interested,' she cut in firmly.

'Bastardising your talent, hm?' he said ruefully.

'Not at all!' Christi was genuinely shocked. 'America has some really talented people. I'm not one of those actors who think the "British theatre",' she affected a haughtily English accent,

'is everything.' She shook her head. 'I just feel...
This is my home,' she shrugged. 'My family—what
little there is—is here.'

'But I thought Dizzy and Zach were your only
family?' Barry frowned. 'And little Laura, of
course.'

Christi gave a puzzled frown. 'They are.'

'Then when they go to the States——'

'What?' She faced him tensely. 'But they aren't
going to the States,' she denied confidently, unnerved by Barry's guilty expression. 'Are they?' she
voiced uncertainly.

'Nothing has been decided yet,' he answered
awkwardly. 'But I've made your uncle an offer for
the film rights to one of his books, with the in-
clusion that he will write the screenplay,' he explained slowly. 'He's still thinking about it.'

No mention of this had been made over the
weekend, not in front of her, anyway. Was she the
reason Zach and Dizzy were hesitating? She knew
her uncle and Dizzy took their responsibility
towards her very seriously, and they wouldn't lightly
view leaving her alone in England for six months
or so. She *would* miss them all, very much, but this
was too good an opportunity for Zach to pass up,
and she would tell him so when she made her weekly
call to them on Sunday evening; to telephone earlier
would be to make too much of their hesitation. She
would just casually mention what a good idea she
thought it was, and leave them to make their decision from there.

'It sounds marvellous!' She gave a brightly encouraging smile. 'Tell me more about it.'

Barry was only too happy to do so, for this was the other 'project' he was working on at the moment. It sounded wonderful, filming beginning early next year if her uncle was agreeable, the deal he was being offered probably enough to renovate the rest of Castle Haven, which was her uncle's lifetime ambition, only having been able to afford the work on the east wing of the rundown castle so far. The thought of leaving her alone in England for all those months *had* to be the reason he was hesitating.

'I'm sure we could find a part for you in the film if it would help Zach to—well——' Barry broke off uncomfortably as she looked at him with raised brows. 'It was only an idea,' he dismissed ruefully.

'I'm as much against nepotism as I am the casting couch,' Christi told him drily.

'That really was dumb of me,' he said with a groan, his adopted American accent more pronounced in his self-disgust. 'I really am sorry,' he grimaced. 'Although the part of the heroine's sister would be perfect—no,' he accepted drily as Christi slowly shook her head. 'Nepotism is a dirty word, right?' he dismissed.

'Right,' she agreed drily.

'But if it were someone else's script—but it isn't,' he sighed as Christi just continued to look at him patiently. 'I've said far too much, probably ruined what has so far been a perfect evening——'

'You haven't ruined it at all,' she assured him lightly, picking up her clutch-bag. 'After all, I asked you to tell me more about it. But it is late now,' she smiled. 'I really should be getting home.'

Barry sighed. 'I *did* ruin the evening——'

'Really—you didn't,' she insisted without rancour. 'I'm grateful that you told me about it.'

'If you're sure...?' He still didn't look convinced, his handsome face set in self-reproachful lines.

'I'm sure.' Christi stood up in one fluid movement, the soft wool of the pale blue dress she wore falling gently against her knees.

It was almost twelve by the time Christi searched for her door-key in her bag. Surely it was far too late to be calling on Lucas. Wasn't it?

'Here, let me.' Barry took the key from her unresisting fingers, deftly unlocking the door for her.

He had certainly had plenty of practice at that, Christi acknowledged warily. Still unmarried, at thirty-six, so perhaps that wasn't so surprising! *Whatever* his experience, he made her nervous.

She turned to face him in the doorway, effectively blocking his entrance. 'Thank you for a lovely evening. The dinner was superb and the show was excellent.' She gave him a glowing smile.

He looked chagrined at the obvious dismissal. And then he relaxed, chuckling softly. 'I guess I've lived in the glitz and glamour of Hollywood too long, where the usual thank you for an enjoyable evening is an equally enjoyable night in bed!'

'I guess you have,' Christi drily mocked him.

Barry shook his head, grinning widely, looking years younger. 'Dizzy told me I was going to like you.'

Christi gave an inclination of her head. 'She told me the same thing about you.'

He looked at her admiringly. 'She wasn't wrong as far as I'm concerned,' he told her huskily.

'Nor me,' she assured softly.

She was ready for his kiss, waiting, her face raised invitingly to his, his mouth firm and warm as it claimed hers.

His mouth moved against hers with expertise, eliciting a response; it was only when his hands began a slow exploration of her body that Christi froze, his caresses an intrusion, an act of theft against the man she really wanted.

Barry drew back ruefully, releasing her slowly. 'Can I see you again?' he prompted gruffly, blue eyes dark with passion. 'Saturday?'

'I—have a date for Saturday.' She couldn't quite meet his gaze.

'Oh, yes,' his voice hardened, 'with David Kendrick, right?'

'Right,' she confirmed uncomfortably. If she'd had Dizzy by her side right now, she would cheerfully have wrung her neck for her, new mother or not! Her friend had put her in such a compromising situation with these three men, that by the time the week was ended probably none of them would even want to talk to her again, let alone have their thoughts on matrimony!

'Then, how about next week?' Barry suggested lightly.

'Er—can I call you?' she prevaricated. 'I'm hoping to have found work by next week, and I'm not sure when or where I'll be working.'

He nodded acceptance. 'You have the number of my hotel. I'll look forward to hearing from you.'

Christi wondered ruefully how long it had been since an evening had ended so tamely for Barry Robbins, as she moved about her kitchen making herself a cup of coffee, having decided it *was* too late to bother Lucas now. The poor man probably hadn't been sent meekly on his way at the end of an evening for years. Oh well, at least he wasn't likely to forget the evening he had spent with her!

She had changed into her nightshirt and was sitting on the sofa, drinking her coffee, when she heard the soft knock on her apartment door.

Barry had seemed to take her refusal good-naturedly, but if he had come back for another try he couldn't have been quite as amiable about it as she had thought he was!

She gaped at Lucas as she peered up at him from around the edge of the door, straightening as she opened it wider.

'Don't look so surprised,' he derided, bending down to pat Henry as the dog yapped about his ankles, demanding attention. 'I think we had better go inside before he wakes our neighbours up,' he suggested ruefully.

Christi stepped back dazedly, following him through to the lounge, drinking her fill of him as,

Henry's feelings appeased, the two cats stretched and purred in the armchair for his attention.

Lucas certainly hadn't been drinking this evening; his hair was neatly combed, his eyes intelligently alert, no lines of bitterness were etched into his face. He had obviously spent the evening relaxing at home; the short-sleeved brown shirt was partly unbuttoned at his throat, faded denims rested low down on lean hips and thighs. It made Christi's breath catch and her palms grow damp just to look at him!

The cats lay on their backs in ecstasy as one leanly muscular hand caressed their silky tummies, and Christi quivered with jealousy as she longed to know the caress of those hands against *her* skin.

At last he straightened, but Christi's fascinated gaze still followed the strength of his hands as he thrust them into his denims' pockets, pulling the material even tighter across his thighs.

'I was waiting for you to come over.' Lucas's quizzical gaze met hers as she at last raised her eyes. He was smiling at her encouragingly. 'When you didn't come, even after you had made yourself a cup of coffee, I decided maybe you thought it was a little late to be making social calls.'

Their kitchens were the only two walls that met in this expensive apartment building and, while they couldn't hear every movement in each other's kitchens, it was possible to tell when an electrical plug had been pushed in. It had disconcerted Christi a little at first, but now she sometimes just sat in her kitchen, listening to the comforting sounds of Lucas moving about next door.

'It *is* after twelve,' she nodded ruefully.

'And we both know you're a nightbird.' Lucas sat down on the sofa, stretching his long legs out in front of him, his hands once again visible as he rested them on the cushions beside him. He relaxed back against the cushions. 'The times we've sat here drinking coffee together when you've returned from the theatre in the evening,' he murmured fondly.

'We went to the theatre tonight,' she rushed into speech, feeling uncomfortable at him having seen her in her nightshirt twice today. It was a dark blue one this time, that made her hair midnight-black and deepened her eyes to almost the same colour. 'To see *Phantom of the Opera*.'

He raised dark brows, stretching up to put his hands behind his head, the power of his chest and shoulders thrown into prominence. 'Good?'

'Very,' she nodded. 'I sometimes wish I could sing; there are so many good musicals about nowadays,' she said wistfully.

'I've heard you in the shower,' Lucas teased. 'I don't think you should inflict your voice on the general public!'

It was incredible how intimately their lives were intertwined; she had heard him singing in the shower once, too, while she'd waited for him to drive her to the theatre one night when her car had broken down. He had a fine baritone which was very pleasing to the ear, whereas she sounded more like Gladys or Josephine in one of their not-so-pleasant moods!

'Probably not,' she agreed lightly.

'Definitely not,' Lucas grinned.

She swallowed hard, somehow feeling at a disadvantage as she stood across the room from him—which was absurd; the person sitting down was usually the one to feel intimidated! 'Did you do anything interesting this evening?' Her lightness of tone didn't reveal her intense interest.

'Oh, no, you don't!' Lucas dismissed laughingly. 'It's your evening we're interested in. The fact that I've been doing paperwork all evening isn't even worth mentioning.'

She shrugged, relieved that his relationship with Michelle seemed to be coming to an end; he had only seen the other woman once this week that she knew of. But once this affair ended there would just be another one, she reminded herself, and one of these times the woman was going to be the right one for Lucas.

'Then we won't mention it.' Christi smiled to hide the nagging pain that thinking of Lucas, finally falling in love, always caused in her heart. 'And I've already told you that my evening went well.'

'No,' he corrected with a shake of his head. 'You said the musical was good. The next relevant question is, was Barry Robbins as good?' he drawled.

'Lucas!' She stared at him with wide eyes.

His mouth twisted. 'As in well behaved,' he explained drily.

'Oh,' she blushed. 'Yes, he was very—well, most of the time—until he brought me home——' She broke off, feeling uncomfortable at the speculative gleam in silver eyes.

'Well, you didn't invite him in, so—— My God, the man didn't try something on the doorstep?' he said disgustedly.

'No, he didn't,' she glared at him indignantly, finding his curiosity about her dates deeply embarrassing. 'He kissed me, that's all,' she told him defensively.

'And?' Lucas looked at her interestedly.

Christi gave a pained frown. 'Lucas, I don't think——'

'Tuesday night, you claimed the kiss was the way you knew Dick Crosby wasn't the right man for you. I merely wondered if you had discovered the same thing about Barry Robbins when *he* kissed you,' Lucas shrugged.

Christi stared at him as if she had never seen him before. He *did* remember the other night! It wasn't that he didn't remember what had happened, it wasn't that he was saving her blushes by not mentioning it, he just hadn't mentioned it earlier because what they had shared hadn't been important to him!

Her family and friends, Lucas among them, all knew that she was usually slow to anger, that it took a great deal to make her angry, but, for possibly the first time in her life, red-hot anger coursed through her like a tidal wave.

How dared Lucas feel nothing after those impassioned kisses they had shared! How *dared* he!

'No,' she replied tautly. 'Barry's kisses were very sensual, very enjoyable,' she told him challengingly.

Lucas's arms slowly lowered to his sides. 'Then, he is the man for you?' he said softly.

Her head was back in proud defiance. 'I didn't say that,' she bit out waspishly. How *dared* he!

Lucas looked puzzled. 'But you said——'

'His kisses were very sensual.' She nodded acknowledgment. 'It was when he began to touch me that I froze,' she shrugged dismissively, her expression deliberately bland.

Lucas sat forward. 'When he—touched, you?' His eyes were narrowed. 'Are you telling me that he tried to make love to you while the two of you were standing in the hallway?' he rasped.

Christi was glad he no longer found this amusing; she had ceased finding it funny a long time ago! 'Hardly,' she derided mockingly. 'He just touched me, that's all. Ran his hands over my body,' she enlarged as Lucas still looked puzzled.

His mouth thinned into a taut line. 'And?'

She shrugged again. 'I didn't like it.'

Lucas frowned darkly. 'What exactly did he do to you?'

Christi looked thoughtful. 'Well, he put his hand here,' she placed her own hand just under her left breast, 'and here,' she placed her other hand on her hip, 'and here,' she moved her right hand slightly higher against her breast. 'And then he—it's a bit awkward for me to show you like this.' She shook her head.

Lucas stood up and came to stand just in front of her, holding out his own hands. 'Show me now,' he invited gruffly.

She didn't hesitate, she was so angry with him for putting her through the torment of the last two days that, at that moment, she didn't *care* if he never spoke to her again after tonight!

She took his left hand and placed it on the curve of her bottom, placing his right hand exactly where hers had been seconds earlier. And the sensation was nothing like the aversion she had felt when Barry had attempted to touch her so intimately. Her whole body started to tingle, Lucas's hands burning her through the silky material of her nightshirt.

'Now what?' Lucas prompted harshly.

Christi looked up at him; she was tall herself, but Lucas easily towered over her. 'It's difficult to remember, really,' she said breathlessly, her nipples already taut against silk. 'He was kissing me, you see,' she shrugged. 'And his hands just sort of— roamed at will.'

'At will,' Lucas echoed tightly, pulling her hard against him, bending his head to claim her mouth in a searing kiss.

At first, she was so lost in the power of that kiss that she wasn't aware of his hands against her body, but as his fingertips caressed the length of her spine she became very aware of that touch, gasping out loud as one of his hands moved to fully cup her breast. Being tall as she was, it would have been nice to be blessed with big breasts, but she hadn't been, and as her breast perfectly fitted into the palm of Lucas's hand she knew why she hadn't: her body had been perfectly fashioned to match and fit his.

All the time he caressed her, that punishing kiss went on, and on, and on . . .

Christi felt weak, clinging to the width of his shoulders, trembling anew as Lucas pulled her thighs tightly against his, at the same time as his lightly caressing tongue stopped playing with her lips and plunged into the waiting warmth beneath.

She felt claimed, possessed, giving a little whimper from too much pleasure all at once, as expert fingers parted her nightshirt all the way down the front, a thumb-tip moving erotically against the hardened tip of her breast.

His denims and shirt were another erotic abrasion against her naked flesh, and she felt herself filled with a moist ache as her body prepared to fully accept him, her limbs trembling expectantly.

She desperately drew air into her ragged lungs as Lucas's mouth left hers to travel the length of her throat, knowing another kind of desperation as that moist mouth claimed the aching tip of her other breast, one hand moving up automatically to thread her fingers through the darkness of his hair as she held him against her, the suckling pressure against her breast deepening the ache between her thighs.

Lucas had gone way beyond any caresses Barry Robbins might have attempted, but Christi didn't want to stop him; she wanted it all, wanted this ache taken away, replaced by the fulfilment she had always known only one man could give her. This man.

The gentle curve of her breast thrust forward moistly as Lucas's mouth left the creamy peak to travel slowly across the silky flesh.

It wasn't until she felt Lucas's fingers deftly re-buttoning her nightshirt that Christi realised his kiss was no longer passionate but soothing, lacking the fire that seconds ago had pulled them both towards the edge of oblivion.

Her body once again covered by blue silk, Lucas raised tender hands to smooth back the dark swathe of her hair from her flushed face. 'And you knew from the way Robbins touched you that he wasn't the man for you?' he prompted huskily.

'Yes,' she breathed shakily, waiting for his obvious conclusion after her response to *him*. Waiting. And waiting.

She was still waiting, minutes later, when Lucas had wished her a gentle goodnight and quietly left to return to his own apartment!

CHAPTER FOUR

CHRISTI had a job. Possibly not the sort of job she would have chosen for herself, given a choice. But the screen test she had had at the beginning of the week had paid off—she was now the glamour in an advertisement for a new liqueur the company intended televising in time for Christmas.

It was a job for a model, of course, although some people said she had the height and looks of a model, anyway, and there was some acting involved, according to the director. And it would mean her face would be seen by millions all over the country, possibly the world, if they chose to syndicate it, as they were doing with so many advertisements nowadays.

They were going to film four different adverts, starting next month, which was only a couple of weeks away, after all. Apparently the company had been searching for just the right girl for months now; it had just been a lucky chance that her agent had sent her along to them. A lucky chance for all of them. At least now she could encourage Dizzy and Zach to take up the opportunity in America, while being able to assure them that she was working and would be fine during their absence.

Ordinarily, she would have shared something like this with Lucas, would have gone over to his apartment as soon as he had got in from work and taken him out for a celebratory dinner.

But nothing was ordinary between herself and Lucas any more. For one thing, she no longer understood him, let alone what was going on between them.

They had lived next door to each other for four years—*four years*—and not once had Lucas shown more than a brotherly interest in her life. In the last four days, she had been in his arms twice, and both times he could have made love to her with no argument from her. And his response to her certainly hadn't been anything but that of a lover.

But the first time he had kissed her Lucas had been demonstrating how a man *should* kiss a woman he desired, and last night he had been pretending he was *another man* making love to her. Where things stood between herself and *Lucas* she had no idea!

However, if the last four days hadn't happened, Lucas was the person she would have wanted to celebrate with, and if he could face her as if the other night hadn't happened she, supposedly the trained actress of the two of them, could surely face him as if last night hadn't happened! Even if she, and her body, could remember every kiss, every caress...

Knowing that Fridays were always especially busy for Lucas, working later than usual before the office closed down for the weekend, Christi was aware that he rarely, if ever, made a date for that evening, so he should be free later on to help her celebrate.

Booking a table at their favourite restaurant
should be an easy matter; in the past, she had
always just had to mention Lucas's name and the
table was arranged as if by magic. The man-
agement must wonder at her appearance every few
months or so, after the beauties who usually accompanied him for a few weeks, before disappearing, never to be seen with him again!

She spoke to Simon, the *maître d'*, when she got
through to the restaurant, mentioning that the table
would be for Lucas Kingsley.

'But Mr Kingsley already has a reservation for
nine-thirty,' he assured her.

Christi frowned. 'Are you sure?' What a silly
question! If Simon said Lucas had a reservation,
then that was exactly what he had; Simon was so
good at his job, the restaurant ran like a well-oiled
machine.

'Very sure, madam.' There was only a slight
frosting to the confirmation.

Lucas already had a date for tonight, after all.
'How silly of me,' she said in a hollow voice. 'There
must have been some confusion over who was to
book the table,' she excused lamely, hoping this
man didn't choose to mention the supposed 'mix-
up' to Lucas, or his partner for the evening, when
they arrived there later!

'Yes, madam,' Simon returned politely.

Christi replaced the receiver slowly, a dejected
droop to her shoulders. Lucas must be seeing
Michelle tonight, after all. So much for the relationship coming to an end! It was only on special

occasions, and for special women, that Lucas broke his rule about keeping Friday evenings free to relax.

She looked down at the petrol-blue dress she wore, a silky shimmer of material that clung alluringly to her curved body, a perfect foil for her dark hair. She felt like Cinderella in reverse; all dressed up and nowhere to go!

She was still debating whether to change and spend the evening quietly at home—if it could be called quiet when the cats and Henry seemed to be going through one of their squabbling nights!—or whether to call up a couple of friends and do her celebrating with them, when she heard Lucas outside in the corridor.

It wouldn't hurt just to pop over for a few minutes to tell him about the job, now would it? Why was she trying to talk herself into it when she knew it was what she really wanted to do?

Her bright smile of greeting died on her lips as the door to Lucas's apartment was opened by none other than—*Marsha Kingsley*!

Christi stared at her in some disbelief. Visiting Lucas once in a week to talk about the welfare of their children seemed perfectly natural to her, but for the other woman to be here *twice* . . .

A slow smile spread over Marsha's mocking features, her eyes appearing catlike in their pleasure. 'Well, well!' She looked Christi up and down speculatively. 'Little girl going out to play, is she?'

If this woman had been anyone other than Lucas's ex-wife, Christi would have been able to handle the sarcasm, but it was because Marsha *had* once been married to Lucas, had known him more intimately for four years than any other person, that Christi at once felt at a disadvantage whenever she met her. And, of course, she *was* at a disadvantage; Lucas had once loved this woman enough to marry her.

'I'm going out later, yes,' she answered abruptly. 'Is——'

'With the man from the other evening?' Marsha drawled. 'Dick something-or-other?'

'Crosby,' she supplied tersely. 'And no, it isn't. Is Lucas—'

'At home?' the other woman finished softly. 'But, of course. He's just taking a shower,' she murmured throatily. 'Your men may have matured slightly, but *you* obviously haven't—not enough to keep them interested, anyway,' she added tauntingly.

Christi drew in an angry breath, hating this woman's derision, *furiously angry* at Lucas's easy familiarity of taking a shower with his ex-wife in his apartment. Just what was going on? 'Experience may count for something,' she snapped. 'But experience is something I'll attain. Youth is something *you'll* never see again!'

She hadn't meant to say that, bitchiness had never been one of her weaknesses. But from the furious glitter in Marsha's suddenly venomous eyes she knew she had surpassed herself at her first attempt!

She gave a weary sigh. 'I didn't come here to fight with you——'

'Then why did you come?' Marsha challenged harshly. 'To try and convince Lucas you're all grown up at last?' she scorned. 'Don't look so stricken,' she taunted as Christi paled. 'I guessed from the beginning that you imagined yourself in love with Lucas. But you're a child to him, you always will be.' She gave a derisive laugh. 'You could dance naked on a table-top and he would probably just offer you his jacket so that you didn't catch cold!'

It wasn't true ... yet, wasn't it the same thing, but put in a different way, that she had been telling herself for years?

Even after Tuesday and Thursday nights? But she already knew that she had provoked him on both those occasions. And that afterwards Lucas had acted as if nothing unusual had happened. He probably just put it down as a further step in her education on his part!

'I don't know what Lucas ever saw in you!' she choked, her nails digging into her palms.

Marsha's mouth twisted. 'Give yourself another ten years or so and you'll know,' she mocked.

'Sex isn't everything!' Christi denied in a pained voice.

Marsha gave a derisive shrug. 'With a man like Lucas, it isn't nothing, either.'

Christi swallowed the nausea that rose up in her throat at the thought of Lucas with this woman. 'How fortunate for him that he's become more discriminating over the years!' she bit out with distaste.

Marsha was completely in control again now, her brief show of anger masked behind mockery. 'Has he?' she challenged softly.

She could feel the colour drain completely out of her cheeks. Marsha couldn't be saying—Lucas wouldn't—he *couldn't*——

But Lucas had cared for this woman once, had children with her, and it had never been his decision to end their marriage. Despite his bitterness about the way things had ended between them, Lucas had never once claimed to hate his ex-wife for what she had done.

Lucas and Marsha...

Christi readily admitted that during this last week, the man she had thought she had known for the last four years had seemed like a stranger to her at times, a man who looked like Lucas but who certainly didn't act like him. Would his having an affair with Marsha be any more difficult to comprehend than the occasions he had taken *her* into his arms the last week?

Lucas and Marsha...

Oh, God, she didn't want to believe that! This woman entwining her body around his like a sensuous cat——

'We always were pretty explosive in bed together,' Marsha taunted softly at Christi's obvious growing horror. 'Why don't you ask him? No, I don't suppose you'll do that, will you?' she derided with mockery. 'If it's any consolation, Christi, you could *never* hope to keep a man like Lucas satisfied.'

Christi wanted to wipe the knowing smile off the other woman's red-painted lips, wanted to deny the hurtful claim. But Lucas *hadn't* wanted her enough, on either of the occasions she had been in his arms, to lose his icy control and make love to her.

Oh, God, a week ago her life had been tranquil and secure, even if the man she was in love with had never been able to return those feelings. Now she wasn't sure what she and Lucas had any more, and he seemed to be involved with this—this——

'You really are so transparent.' Marsha gave a husky laugh. 'Maybe Lucas should have done you both a favour and put you out of your misery years ago; a brief affair would certainly have been kinder than fending off your adolescent devotion with brotherly affection all these years,' she dismissed in a bored voice.

Lucas didn't know how she felt about him, he couldn't know! *Why* couldn't he? a voice murmured inside her; this woman seemed to have had no trouble guessing at her love for him! Oh God!

'Marsha, I thought I heard——' Lucas broke off frowningly as he saw the two of them standing together in the doorway. He finished tying the belt to his robe as he straightened questioningly. 'Christi,' he greeted lightly.

Christi felt as if he had struck her a blow. Lucas was obviously naked beneath the bathrobe, and he had walked into the room to be with his ex-wife dressed that way, his hair still damp from the shower he had just taken.

Marsha had been telling the truth about that. And Christi had a sinking feeling that the other woman had been telling the truth about a lot of other things, too.

Her head went back defensively. 'I was just on my way out.' Amazingly, her voice didn't tremble and shake as she had feared it would! 'And I just thought I would let you know I've found a job.'

'That's great,' he said with genuine pleasure.

'Yes,' she agreed tersely, keeping her gaze averted from his dark masculinity. 'I didn't realise at the time that I would be interrupting anything——'

'But——'

'I really do have to go now, Lucas,' she continued brittly as he would have interrupted. 'I hope you both have a nice evening,' she added tautly, turning away.

'But, Christi——'

'Leave her alone, Lucas,' Marsha chided throatily. 'Can't you see the poor girl has more on her mind than talking to us?'

Christi heard the door close softly behind her, and she didn't need to turn to know that both Marsha and Lucas were still on the other side of it. She couldn't allow herself to think what they would be doing in a couple of minutes from now!

Marsha was wrong, very wrong; the *only* thing Christi had on her mind was Lucas and her. Together.

She closed her eyes, tears squeezing out between the lids.

She would have to keep to that decision she had made on Wednesday about moving. She couldn't go on living here now that Lucas was seeing Marsha, now that she knew he had realised all the time that she was in love with him.

She felt so humiliated. So hurt. So betrayed.

She hadn't been able to help loving Lucas. But he was so much older than her, so much wiser, couldn't he have found some way over the years to let her know, gently, that he realised how she felt but that there could be no future for them?

Maybe she was being unfair, the onus hadn't been on Lucas to deal with the problem at all, but on her. She had always known there could never be anything between them, she had just refused to accept it.

Well, now she accepted it! She loved Lucas, but her feelings were an embarrassment to him. She couldn't change the way she felt about him, she doubted she would ever be able to do that, but she could remove the embarrassment, herself, from his life.

Christi had wanted so badly to get out of her date for this evening, she had telephoned Dizzy to ask for David Kendrick's telephone number, only to find, when she called his home, that David wasn't at home to answer her repeated calls, but seemingly out for the day.

She looked terrible, and she felt even worse. She had crept quietly back into her apartment last night, so that neither Lucas nor Marsha should realise she was hiding away like a wounded animal rather than going out as they had expected her to do.

She had heard the other couple leaving just after nine o'clock. Finally, she'd been able to move about freely, yet she'd still been sitting dazedly in an armchair when she had heard Lucas's return. She'd given a nervous start when his gentle knock had sounded on the door, instantly silencing Henry with a raised warning finger, as he would have barked excitedly at the familiar knock.

She had trembled when Lucas had called to her softly through the closed door, knocking again, a little louder this time, almost as if he'd sensed her watchfulness behind the wooden barrier. Again she'd silenced Henry, waiting tensely for the sound of Lucas going to his own apartment, her breath leaving her body in a shaky sigh when he had finally done so.

Christi hadn't dreamt such misery existed; not even her regrets after Tuesday evening had been as bad as this raw pain. The last thing she wanted was to move away from Lucas, but what if his relationship with Marsha deepened, became serious? What if they decided to remarry?

Lucas had left his apartment shortly before David called for her, and she could only guess that his companion for the evening was Marsha. Oh, God, just the thought of them together...

Her deep sigh of despair didn't go unnoticed by her companion. David smiled enquiringly. He was a tall, dark-haired man with laughing blue eyes and a lithe attraction which must have set many female hearts fluttering over the years. And which left Christi unmoved.

'Penny for them?' he encouraged at her silence.

She gave a wan smile. 'I'm afraid they aren't even worth that,' she dismissed wearily. 'I'm sorry I'm not better company. I did try to call you today to cancel our dinner date, but——'

'I've been out of town,' he nodded comprehendingly. 'I spent the day with Dizzy and Zach.'

'What?' That shook her out of her despondency. If David had been in the Lake District with Dizzy and Zach when she'd called, then Dizzy had deliberately not told her so! And she didn't need two guesses why; Dizzy had obviously guessed that the reason she wanted David's number had been because she wanted to cancel their date. And she had effectively balked her plans.

Damn Dizzy and her matchmaking! But for her friend's interference, she needn't have put David or herself through the unnecessary awkwardness of tonight. Although, she had to admit, David didn't seem too disturbed by her lack of enthusiasm for the evening. And she didn't for one moment believe it was a reaction he usually got from his dates. He was the sort of man to have women flocking around him, not the sort who had to try and cajole one insipidly reluctant woman into having a good time!

She readily admitted she wasn't looking her best tonight; the strain of the last week was beginning to tell on her, obvious by the dark shadows in and below her eyes, and the fact that her expression was lacking its usual sparkle. If things deteriorated any further, she was going to lose that advertising job before they even began filming!

'Did Dizzy forget to mention that?' David looked amused at her chagrin. He relaxed back in his chair, their meal over, Christi's barely touched. 'I suppose she thought it only fair that I should at least be given a chance to talk you around.'

'Around to what?' Christi gave him a curious frown; if he was trying to talk her into going to bed with him, it was the most direct approach she had heard yet!

'Into talking to Zach about writing the screenplay for his book so that Barry could make it into a film,' David told her shruggingly.

Christi stared at him as if she had never seen him before, going to speak twice before changing her mind, then finally swallowing hard. 'Is that what—— Were Dick and Barry——'

'Not very subtly trying to do that?' he finished amiably. 'Yes,' he confirmed drily.

She remembered now how Dick had changed the conversation at her lack of attention, claiming he must be boring her, how Barry had even offered her a part in the film as an inducement to persuading Zach into working on the script.

Her mouth tightened. 'Then why aren't you going to try, too,' she snapped with distaste.

He shrugged again. 'Dick doesn't know Zach very well, his main interest is in promoting Dizzy's work through the film. Barry may have known Zach years ago, but he doesn't know him too well now,' he said ruefully. 'On the other hand, I know Zach well enough to realise that only Zach will make his mind up about the filming of one of his books. And that's where the problem comes in; Zach isn't too thrilled at the idea of his identity as Claudia Laurence becoming public.'

She could imagine that her very private uncle wouldn't! 'Am I to take it by your admissions that *your* interest in me is the real thing?' Christi's voice dripped sarcasm.

David smiled at her obvious anger. 'The last woman I tried to deceive punched me in the eye—and then a week later she married me,' he recalled with obvious pleasure.

Christi gaped at him. 'You're *married*?' She was sure Dizzy couldn't have known *that* when she encouraged Christi to go out with him!

'Not any more,' he said regretfully. 'Sara died.'

'I'm so sorry,' Christi gasped, knowing David's simply made statement in no way reflected the pain that suddenly clouded his eyes.

'I'm sorry she died,' he nodded, looking older than his thirty-three years now that there was no laughter in his face. 'But I'm not sorry that I knew her, that I loved her, even if it was only for a very brief time,' he announced with feeling. 'The tabloids are always speculating as to why I haven't married again.' He pulled a face. 'I don't think any of them would understand if I said I've had my love and she's irreplaceable.'

Christi felt like crying, ashamed of her own self-pity tonight. Lucas might be out of her reach, but at least he was alive, at least she was able to *look* at him and know that she loved him!

'Irreplaceable, yes,' she clasped David's hand across the table, 'but, as that old saying goes, "when one door closes another one opens". The door on your love for Sara has closed, David,' she said softly. 'But there is room in your heart for someone else, I'm sure of it.'

He turned his hand over, taking her hand into his, gently smoothing the delicate skin there. 'You?' he prompted huskily.

'No,' she said regretfully.

He gave a rueful smile, releasing her hand. 'I didn't think so,' he accepted without rancour. 'Does Dizzy know about this man in your life?'

She didn't question how he knew she was in love with someone else; she had greatly underestimated this man, believed him to be something of a playboy, when he was really gentle and kind, with a perception beyond words. 'No,' she sighed.

'I didn't think so,' he smiled, the sadness fading from his eyes. 'If she did, Dick, Barry and I wouldn't have been the ones invited for last weekend,' he mocked.

'And Dizzy would be making my life more miserable than it already is!' she grimaced.

David gave her a searching look. 'You mean,' he said slowly, 'this man doesn't return your feelings?' He looked disbelieving.

'Doesn't return them. Doesn't *want* them,' she added, bitter at the way Lucas had let her continue to make a fool of herself all these years. She felt so *angry* at the way he must have been humouring her all this time. Just like the child he still believed her to be...

A *child*? My God, she was almost twenty-two years old, and a lot of women were married with children by this age. The majority of her friends were, for a start, including Dizzy. Damn Lucas and his patronising gentleness; it was the last thing she wanted from him!

'The man's a fool,' David murmured across the table from her.

'Yes,' she said firmly. 'Yes, he is,' she dismissed.

David grinned appreciatively. 'Do I detect a spark of rebellion in those amazing blue eyes?' he teased.

'You most certainly do,' she acknowledged with satisfaction.

'Going to give him hell, hmm?' he said ruefully.

Christi gave a rueful shake of her head. 'I'm going to give him nothing, David,' she stated flatly. 'I thought he was my friend, but——' She shrugged dismissively. 'Now I just feel a fool for loving him all this time.' She sighed.

David's expression gentled. 'I'm afraid that making a fool of yourself is part of being in love,' he told her softly. 'Take the word of the man who was still sporting the black eye at his wedding that his bride had given him at their very first meeting!'

Christi's mouth quirked. 'I'd really like to hear about this courtship some time.' She smiled her amusement at the idea of any woman punching this man in the eye, let alone marrying him a week later!

He chuckled. 'And I'd enjoy telling it to you. But there's no rush,' he said confidently. 'I have the feeling you and I are going to be good friends.'

She did too, and this would be a genuine friendship, with no deeper love hidden on either side. She couldn't help but admire David's frankness in explaining to her how much he had loved his wife, how much he still loved her. If nothing else, she should thank Dizzy for introducing her to a new friend.

'Let's go and have a brandy at my apartment,' she suggested impulsively as they were asked if they wanted a liqueur after their coffee.

David nodded dismissively to the waiter. 'Sounds like a good idea,' he told Christi warmly, holding her arm lightly as they stood up to leave.

David kept up a light conversation as he drove them both to her apartment, Christi as relaxed in his company as she used to be in Lucas's—before things had changed so drastically between them.

Thinking of Lucas sobered her, and she was very quiet as they went up to her apartment. She couldn't help wondering if Lucas had bothered to keep to his unspoken rule of not bringing women back to his apartment for the night. Did the same rule still apply when the woman was your ex-wife? she wondered bitterly.

'If you've had second thoughts about the brandy——'

'Certainly not!' Christi roused herself, smiling brightly, realising what rotten company she had been the last few minutes. She put her arm companionably through the crook of David's. 'I'm hoping to persuade you to tell me all about what sounds like an explosive courtship,' she confided with relish, unlocking her door.

David grinned. 'I——'

'Christi, I want—oh!' A stony-faced Lucas came to an abrupt halt in the doorway of his apartment as he saw she wasn't alone. 'Kendrick,' he greeted icily.

'Hello, Lucas,' David returned speculatively. 'I had no idea you lived in this apartment building, too.' He eyed the other man questioningly.

'There's no reason why you should have known,' Lucas rasped, his expression cold.

Christi had been struck dumb as soon as Lucas had put in his unexpected appearance. His bow-tie had been removed, his snowy-white shirt was partly unbuttoned at the neck, black evening trousers tailored to his lean waist and thighs. Was Marsha waiting in his apartment even now for him to rejoin her? What could be so important to say to her that he had interrupted his evening with the other woman, anyway?

'No,' David accepted lightly, lean fingers covering Christi's as her hand had tightened convulsively on his arm at her first sight of Lucas. 'Nice to have seen you again. If you'll excuse us?' he effectively dismissed the other man.

Lucas's mouth thinned, his eyes narrowed to icy slits. 'Christi, I want to talk to you,' he told her tightly.

She had regained much of the composure she had lost when he'd appeared so suddenly, her gaze direct and unblinking. 'Can't it wait until morning?' she dismissed coolly. 'David and I were just about to have a—nightcap.' She was deliberately provocative in her claim, sensing David's amusement at her side. He really was the *nicest* man.

Lucas's expression became thunderous as he drew in a controlling breath. 'I really think it would be better if we talked right now,' he bit out with abrupt precision.

'You——'

'Why don't I go and wait in your apartment for you, Christi?' David suggested lightly, patting her hand encouragingly. 'After all,' he added mockingly, 'we have all night; I'm sure we can spare Lucas a few minutes of your time.'

Christi shot him a grateful look, her smile fading and her eyes hardening as she turned back to Lucas. 'I'll just be a few moments,' she told him coldly. 'If you would like to wait in your own apartment?' she added pointedly, as he stood watching them.

He turned abruptly on his heel and slammed the door behind him.

'So much for consideration for our neighbours,' Christi muttered as she followed David into the apartment, her gaze averted in embarrassed awkwardness as she introduced him to Henry, Gladys and Josephine, her hands trembling as she poured him the promised brandy.

David moved to stand behind her, his hands coming down to rest comfortingly on her shoulders.

'We can talk about him or not, Christi,' he assured her gently. 'Whatever you're comfortable with, OK?' He looked down at her encouragingly as he turned her to face him.

She closed her eyes, biting her bottom lip to stop it trembling, tears shimmering in her eyes as she raised her lids. 'Maybe later,' she offered ruefully.

He squeezed her shoulders reassuringly. 'Whatever,' he repeated softly.

She drew in a ragged breath. 'I'd better go and see what he wants.'

David grinned, releasing her. 'From the smoke coming out of his ears when he saw me with you, I would say the first thing he'll do is warn you what a bad boy I am,' he said self-derisively.

'Whereas you're really just a nice man who has offered to be my friend,' she reminded defensively.

'Don't tell Lucas that!' he warned, scandalised. 'My reputation will be in shreds if it gets around I've been offering nothing but friendship to a beautiful woman!'

Christi chuckled at his nonsense. 'I promise not to tell him,' she said drily.

He laughed softly. 'I didn't think you would!'

They shared a smile of complete understanding; she no more wanted Lucas to know that yet *another* handsomely devastating man had been unable to offer her more than friendship, than David wanted it to be public knowledge that no woman had meant anything to him since Sara, his wife.

David settled down in an armchair, the two cats instantly vying for position on his lap, David watching them bemusedly. 'If you need any help next door just shout,' he offered absently.

Her mouth set determinedly. 'I may not be the one shouting for help!'

He grinned appreciatively. 'Lucas is big enough to take care of himself,' he dismissed, sipping his brandy unconcernedly.

Christi didn't even bother to knock on the door of the apartment next door; if Lucas had Marsha in there with him, that was his fault!

He was alone in the lounge, his face looking as if it were carved from granite, watching her approach with narrowed silver eyes.

Christi stopped several feet away, facing him defiantly. 'I have someone waiting for me,' she finally reminded harshly as he made no attempt to speak.

A nerve pulsed in Lucas's jaw. 'Waiting for what?' he rasped. 'Christi,' his voice softened as she gave an outraged gasp, 'I respect and admire David Kendrick immensely as a businessman, but as a man——'

'As a man, you think he's nothing but a user of women,' she finished furiously. 'I suppose *you* would know all about men like that.'

Lucas's face darkened ominously. 'What the hell is that supposed to mean?'

Christi eyed him contemptuously. 'Where is Marsha—waiting for you in the bedroom?'

'Marsha?' he frowned. 'But——'

'Don't tell me.' She held up silencing hands. 'I'm not interested in whether you intend making love to your ex-wife here or back at her home. What I do object to is your thinking you have some right to make judgements about the people in *my* life!' Her eyes glittered angrily.

'David Kendrick in particular?' he said, his voice dangerously soft.

'Yes,' she challenged, her head back proudly. 'I've only been out with him one evening, but I already know he's a man I can admire and respect—in every way!'

Lucas drew in a harshly furious breath. 'Enough to go to bed with him?'

'That's my business.' Her voice had risen angrily, for she was more furious than she could ever remember before, with an anger that had been building since yesterday, ever since she had found Marsha in Lucas's apartment for the second time in a week. 'You stay out of my life, Lucas,' she snapped. 'And I'll stay out of yours!'

'But Kendrick is a——'

'Stay out of my life, Lucas,' she warned, her eyes flashing.

'He passed the kissing and caressing test with honours, did he?' Lucas grated harshly.

'Oh, definitely,' she bit out challengingly.

A spasm moved in his throat. 'Then that leaves only one last test left,' he muttered grimly.

'Exactly,' she acknowledged brittly. 'Now if this conversation is over——'

'Christi!' Lucas grasped her arm as she would have turned away. 'Don't do this!' he compelled.

'Don't you think he'll be an experienced enough teacher for me?' she scorned.

He breathed raggedly. 'Don't make your first time with a man an act of defiance against me,' he pleaded softly. 'If I've interfered too much in your life, then I'm sorry, but please don't——'

'You arrogant b——!' She broke off disgustedly, flinching out of his grasp. 'My being with David will have *nothing* to do with you,' she bit out between clenched teeth. 'Now this conversation is definitely over!'

'Christi——'

She turned at the door, her eyes dull with pain. 'It's over, Lucas,' she told him bitterly. 'Whatever it was between us—friendship, tolerance?' She shrugged dismissively. 'It's over.'

She closed the door softly behind her, remembering what she had told David earlier this evening about doors opening and closing. The door in her life behind which Lucas stood was definitely closed. For ever.

CHAPTER FIVE

'FEELING better today?'

Christi gave a shaky smile at David's gentle query. She had remained completely calm on Saturday night until she had reached the sanctuary of her apartment, and then the enormity of what she'd done had washed over her and she had buried her face in David's shoulder as she'd sobbed out every angry tear. And they had become the cleansing tears to ease her pain. Except the pain hadn't gone away, a dull ache still in her chest.

David had been wonderful that night, holding her until the tears had stopped, gently washing her face, asking no questions, but helping her slip off her dress before putting her in her bed, kissing her lightly on the brow before inviting her out to lunch on Monday.

She had fallen into an exhausted sleep once he'd left, completely drained emotionally. She had barely moved from her bed on Sunday, although she had heard Lucas moving about in the apartment next door. Knowing he was so close, and yet unreachable to her, had made her feel even worse, and she'd resolved to start looking for somewhere else to live on Monday.

But at least she had managed to set Dizzy and Zach's minds at rest about her immediate future when she had made her customary call to them last night, managing to instil enthusiasm into her voice as she'd told them of the advertising campaign she was involved in and of her friendship with David, sure that it would help Zach in his decision about the film rights to his book, no matter what David thought to the contrary.

David. He really was the nicest man she had ever met. Except Lucas. Oh, damn Lucas, and the hold he had over her heart and her life! If it weren't for her love for him, she *might* have been the one to open that other door in David's heart. She was sure she would at least have wanted to try.

Her smile was wan. 'Not really,' she sighed heavily.

David shook his head. 'I didn't think you would be. You've loved him for a very long time, haven't you?'

'That shows too, does it?' she grimaced.

'No.' He clasped her hand across the table. 'I just remembered after I left you on Saturday night that Lucas was with you at Dizzy and Zach's wedding last year. I remembered thinking at the time that if Lucas weren't careful *he* would be the one standing before an altar before too long. With you at his side,' he explained gently.

'As you see,' Christi's voice was brittle, 'he was very careful!' She gave a self-derisive laugh. 'I never even had a chance with him. Never!' she repeated disgustedly.

'He's a lot older than you——'

'Not another one obsessed with age!' she scorned impatiently.

He quirked dark brows. 'Lucas has mentioned that too, has he?' he said slowly.

She sighed irritably. 'He never ceases reminding me that he's thirty-seven, and, if not actually old enough to be my father, at least old enough to be an uncle or much older brother. I already have an uncle, and I've never wanted a brother!'

David's mouth twisted. 'I doubt if Lucas particularly wanted a niece or a sister, either!'

'Then why relegate me to those roles?' she derided.

He shrugged. 'Protection?'

'From me?' She nodded dully. 'Yes,' she sighed. 'It was certainly one way of avoiding any embarrassing declarations of love from me.'

'That wasn't quite what I meant——'

'Oh, believe me, David,' she said wearily. 'I know what I'm talking about.' She clearly remembered every humiliating detail of that conversation with Marsha on Friday night.

David whistled through his teeth. 'That was certainly some argument you and Lucas had on Saturday night! I gather you haven't spoken to each other since—no,' he answered his own question at her derisive expression. 'From the shouting I heard through the walls, I would say the two of you had said enough. What can I say?' He held up defensive hands as she raised questioning brows. 'I was wandering around your kitchen when I realised that, although I couldn't hear what was being said, I could definitely hear your raised voices.'

Christi sighed. 'You're lucky that's all you heard,' she derided. 'For a brief moment, after I had told Lucas I intended going to bed with you, I thought he was going to hit me.' She could still clearly remember that convulsive spasm in Lucas's throat, the tightening of his hands into fists.

David gave a choked laugh. 'I'm not surprised. What I want to know is, what changed your mind between his apartment and yours?' he leered.

His teasing eased her tension, and she found herself returning his smile. 'I hope you don't mind my using you in that way,' she said apologetically. 'I was just so angry...'

'What man could possibly mind being thought worthy of taking a beautiful woman like you to bed?' He squeezed her hand reassuringly.

'Lucas, to name but one,' she returned drily. 'Oh, why does he have to enter into the conversation all the time?' she said exasperatedly. 'I'm sure you didn't meet me today to talk about him!' she added self-disgustedly.

'Well, actually...'

Christi looked sharply at David, frowning at his rueful expression. 'But I told you on Saturday that Lucas doesn't care for me the way I care for him. There's nothing else to say.'

He gave a gentle smile. 'I told you then, and I'll tell you again now, you don't have to tell me a thing about you and Lucas——'

'Because there's nothing to tell!' she bit out dully.

'I wanted to talk to you about Lucas,' he reproved softly.

Christi's frown deepened. 'I thought the two of your were merely acquaintances?'

David shrugged. 'I think we can actually be classed as casual friends. Our business dealings mean we often meet up, and we seem to go to a lot of the same parties.'

'Probably know a lot of the same women,' she sighed.

His mouth quirked. 'Probably. Although not in the same way,' he added softly.

Christi blushed, giving a self-disgusted sigh. 'I'm sorry.' She shook her head. 'I'm not normally like this,' she excused lamely. 'I'm just so angry with Lucas still that—— But you wanted to tell me something about Lucas,' she encouraged briskly.

David instantly sobered. 'Well, as I said, we go to a lot of the same parties, know a lot of the same people. One of those people is Marsha, his ex-wife,' he added softly.

Christi tensed, drawing a sharp breath into her lungs. 'Oh, yes?' she returned casually, so casually it was obviously a forced reaction.

He grinned. 'And when I say "know", I don't mean biblically,' he derided.

She put her hand on his in silent apology for her earlier remark. 'I realise that,' she said softly.

'Not that Marsha isn't a beautiful woman——'

'I realise that, too,' she interrupted sharply.

David eyed her speculatively. 'Did you also know that the ex-Mrs Kingsley is thinking of marrying again?'

All the colour drained from Christi's cheeks, her eyes wide and haunted. 'Who?' she managed to ask in a hushed voice.

But she didn't really need to ask, *Lucas* was the man Marsha had been seeing all week. God, did Lucas know of the other woman's plans for him? Did he know, and just not care what the other woman had done to him in the past, considered forgiving and forgetting worth having his children back once more? Or—more painful yet—was it possible Lucas did still love the woman who had once been his wife?

'His name is Julian Holland,' David put in softly.

Christi blinked at him dazedly, still lost in thoughts of Lucas remarried to the sensually kittenish Marsha; it made her feel ill!

'The man Marsha is contemplating marrying,' David told her more clearly, 'his name is Julian Holland. He's something important in the diplomatic service,' he added drily. 'Marsha obviously fancies herself as a diplomat's wife.'

Christi stared at him in bewilderment. But it was *Lucas* Marsha had been seeing all week, Lucas she had claimed was her lover. Claimed . . . Oh, God, she hadn't fallen for the oldest trick in the book, had she, her own insecurity where Lucas was concerned making her a prime target for his ex-wife?

'What is it?' David prompted anxiously at her pained groan. 'Do you know him?' he frowned.

'No—but I'm suddenly knowing Marsha a lot better than I would ever have wished to,' she choked disgustedly. 'Oh, my God,' she breathed slowly, a look of horror on her face. 'If Marsha marries this man, that means he will effectively become Daisy and Robin's father.'

'Not legally,' David sighed. 'But in every other way that matters, their day-to-day lives, yes,' he acknowledged heavily.

No wonder Lucas had been drinking on Tuesday night, if Marsha had just told him she intended giving their children a stepfather in the near future! God knew, the woman made it as awkward as possible for Lucas to see his children now, but once she was remarried...

'This must be killing Lucas,' Christi choked, tears in her eyes. 'Eating him up alive!'

David nodded slowly. 'It must be hell for any man put in that position.'

Lucas must be going through hell already, and all she had done the last week was make life even more difficult for him, forcing herself on him, unwittingly taking advantage of his disturbed state, and then telling him to stay out of her life.

Her own hurt feelings no longer seemed important, just as it no longer mattered that Lucas had always known of her love for him. What *was* important was Lucas himself. And at the moment he was very much in need of a friend, of the friendship he had never once denied her.

She looked at David with tear-wet eyes. 'I've been very stupid and selfish, haven't I?' she said self-disgustedly. 'Acting just like that child I keep claiming not to be.' She shook her head dejectedly. 'And now I'm doing it again,' she said self-reproachfully, straightening determinedly. 'Lucas has been my strength over the last four years; now it's my turn to offer him my support.'

David grinned at her. 'If it's any consolation, *I'm* sure you aren't a child.'

She gave him a grateful look. 'Thank you for telling me about Marsha.' Her voice hardened as she spoke of the other woman. 'It explains so many things that have been puzzling me.'

'I thought it might,' he drawled. 'Marsha always reminds me of an octopus, maintaining one tentacle around all the parts of her life, past and present. She and Lucas have been divorced for years, and yet she's never quite let him go.' He shook his head disgustedly.

And obviously the other woman had taken great pleasure in putting him through hell during the last week!

'Would you mind if I didn't stay for dessert?' she told David apologetically. 'I'm really not hungry, and I—I——'

'Have a friend to go and see,' he nodded understandingly. 'I'll give you a call later in the week, maybe we can try for lunch again.'

'I really am sorry, David——'

'Don't be,' he reassured her lightly. 'I envy Lucas like hell,' he said ruefully.

Christi gave a shaky smile, moving to kiss him warmly on the cheek before hurrying from the restaurant. She had to see Lucas, apologise for her behaviour, tell him that she knew all about Marsha's plans to remarry. All she wanted was for them to be friends again, for him to be able to talk to her, the way he used to.

Lucas rented a floor on one of the buildings in the middle of town, having a couple of assistants and their secretaries, as well as his own private secretary, working for him. The outer room was empty when she entered his office, the secretary's desk clear of papers, evidence that she must have gone out for lunch.

How silly of her! It stood to reason that if she had been out to lunch then so were a lot of other people. Lucas included?

She knocked timidly on his office door, opening it to peer inside, expecting the opulence that met her gaze—the luxurious brown and cream décor, the imposing mahogany desk. She was a little unnerved by the man who stood so silently in front of the window that had views over London, the sunshine behind him making it impossible for her to see his expression.

'Lucas?' she said tentatively.

He straightened, stepping away from the sunlight into the room, his strain instantly obvious as the lines about his mouth and eyes could clearly be seen, his mouth set in weary lines. He looked all of his thirty-seven years at that moment, his expression harshly unapproachable.

Nevertheless, Christi knew she had to approach him, that after the other night he wasn't likely to

come to her again. And why should he? She was
the one who had told him to get out of her life and
stay out!

He frowned wearily. 'What can I do for you?'

She wanted so badly to take the pain and despair
out of his eyes, and felt violent towards Marsha for
doing this to him. How badly everyone suffered
after a divorce: the children bewildered because
their parents were no longer together, one of those
parents sad because they were suddenly deprived of
the children they loved. Lucas was the type of man
who wouldn't allow his pain to make him so bitter
he couldn't function without dwelling on the past,
but this last blow seemed to have been one too
many, and Christi felt tears in her own eyes as she
thought of Robin and Daisy being brought up by
any other man but Lucas, possibly learning to call
that man 'Daddy' in time. It wasn't fair, Lucas had
done nothing wrong, he didn't deserve this pain.

But he looked as if her sympathy would be the
'straw that broke the camel's back', as if he would
crack under the strain if she said one word about
Robin and Daisy, and Marsha's remarriage.

She forced a bright smile to her lips. 'I was
shopping—I didn't see anything I liked,' she excused as his brows rose questioningly at her empty
hands. Damn, she may be an actress, but her lies
could certainly do with improving! 'And so I
thought, why don't I go and see if Lucas is free for
lunch?' She looked at him enquiringly, acting as if
she couldn't see his strain. As if she didn't know
every mood change this man made! 'Are you?' she

prompted lightly, knowing she wouldn't be able to eat a thing, but from the look of Lucas he hadn't eaten much at all the last few days; his skin had an unhealthy pallor, adding to his look of strain.

His expression softened slightly. 'I'm not really hungry, Christi, although I do appreciate the thought,' he bit out curtly.

He certainly wasn't going to make this easy for her. And why should he? She had behaved like a shrew on Saturday night, and Lucas hadn't even realised what she was so angry about!

'Oh, come on, Lucas,' she cajoled softly. 'I know I was a bitch on Saturday night, but you know how emotional women get.' She hated it when men put women's emotionalism down to 'that certain time of the month', but, without introducing the subject of Marsha's visits to his apartment, something that was sure to deepen the pain in his already shadowed eyes, she didn't know what else to do! 'And it did seem as if you were treating me a little too much like a child,' she teased.

He held up defensive hands, lithe and attractive in the dark blue suit, although even that seemed a little looser on him than the last time he had worn that particular suit; he *wasn't* eating properly. 'I realised immediately afterwards that I had over-stepped the boundaries of our friendship——'

'We don't have boundaries to our friendship, Lucas,' she cut in sharply.

He sighed, running a hand through the thickness of his hair. 'Every friendship has boundaries,

Christi,' he said heavily. 'And just lately I've been going way too far over ours,' he grated harshly.

The kissing and caressing... But she wouldn't change a moment of those times she had been in his arms, she knew they were possibly the only memories she would ever have. 'Did it seem as if I minded?' she prompted softly.

Lucas drew in a harsh breath. 'That isn't the point,' he rasped. 'I had no right—— Are you and David Kendrick still seeing each other?' He looked at her with narrowed eyes.

After the earlier lie she had told him, she couldn't say she had just had lunch with the other man, but neither could she let him think she had carried out her threat of Saturday night with that 'one final test'!

She gave an exaggerated sigh. 'I think there must be something wrong with me,' she bemoaned. 'Every sexually attractive man I meet offers me friendship, rather than——'

'Kendrick didn't make love to you Saturday night?' Lucas demanded tautly.

She knew David would forgive her for telling the truth, that he was the type of man who really didn't give a damn what people thought about him, or the fact that he had 'offered a beautiful woman only friendship'. 'I told you, he wants to be my friend,' she grimaced. 'You'll have to tell me what my secret is, Lucas—so that I can do something to change it!' she said disgustedly.

He relaxed slightly. 'I'm not sure I want you to do anything to change it,' he told her ruefully. 'I don't think I'm ready to lose my friend just yet,' he shrugged apologetically.

Her expression softened. 'You'll never lose my friendship, Lucas,' she assured him gruffly. 'There may be times when you wish you could, but I'm afraid you're stuck with me for life.'

A nerve pulsed in his jaw. 'Promise?'

Christi flinched inwardly at the loneliness and despair in that question. Strange, she had never thought of Lucas as being lonely before, but after knowing the companionship of a family for those years it must have been difficult for him to adjust to being on his own again. No wonder he had taken such pleasure in being so protective of her the last few years! While the women in his life changed, with regularity, *she* had become the constant in his life; she wasn't about to let him down again!

'I promise.' She put her arm through the crook of his. 'Now, are you going to take me out to lunch or do I have to kidnap you?' she teased to ease his tension.

He gave a rueful smile. 'I'd like to see you try! But I really can't spare the time for lunch today,' he told her regretfully. 'I have an appointment in—ten minutes,' he said, glancing at his wristwatch.

Which meant he wouldn't be bothering to eat lunch at all today, she thought. 'Then I insist you come over for dinner tonight,' she decided firmly. 'Unless—you have a date?' She frowned her sudden uncertainty.

His mouth twisted. 'No date. I'll bring the wine, shall I?'

She smiled her relief at his acceptance. 'Make it champagne,' she encouraged, her eyes alight with mischief. 'We haven't celebrated my new job yet,' she explained at his raised eyebrows.

'So we haven't,' Lucas gave an indulgent smile. 'Champagne it is,' he promised lightly.

Christi reached up the couple of inches it took to put her on the same level as his cheek, allowing herself the indulgence of her lips against the firmness of his skin. 'I'll see you tonight.' She stepped back, her expression deliberately casual. 'About eight o'clock.'

'It's a date,' he nodded as he walked with her to the door.

If only it were! But she had Lucas's friendship back, and that was all that was important.

CHAPTER SIX

AFTER another week of watching Lucas suffer in silence, Christi wasn't so sure of that.

Oh, their friendship seemed to have returned to its previous familiarity, and yet not once had Lucas mentioned to her Marsha's plans to remarry.

He couldn't have forgiven her for her uncharacteristic behaviour last week if he didn't feel he could talk to her about his problems, she decided. And yet he discussed business with her as he usually did, spent a couple of evenings of the next week at her apartment just chatting the way they used to. But there was no mention of Marsha.

Christi didn't know what to do. She was sure the problem was just festering and growing inside him, tearing him apart, but until he spoke to her about it she didn't feel able to offer her sympathy.

She felt sure he would mention something about it when he told her he was having the children on Saturday, a move from the normal weekend he was allowed every month. But, other than inviting her to join them at the coast for the day, he said nothing.

Christi enjoyed Robin and Daisy's company; she couldn't fault the polite, fun-loving children Marsha had brought them up to be, and was easily able to understand Lucas's dilemma when it had come to custody of them and he had realised they would be happier with their mother.

But he couldn't still feel that way, Christi thought as she watched Lucas building sandcastles with the two children. Their relationship was unmistakable—Robin, a seven-year-old version of his father, Daisy, a feminine version of Lucas, too, obviously going to be a beauty in the years to come. She was sure Lucas couldn't bear the idea of giving their upbringing into another man's care. They were such adorable children, so spontaneously affectionate, that she just wanted to take them home so that Lucas could have them with him always. And she knew he had to feel the same way; she hadn't missed the sadness in his eyes, when he thought no one was looking, as he gazed at his children.

'Will you come and help me, Christi?' Daisy asked in her shy little voice, standing in front of Christi with her bucket and spade, a little frill around the bottom of her flowered bathing costume. 'Daddy and Robin have challenged us to a sandcastle contest.'

'Of course I'll help you.' She reached up to hug the little girl, her breath catching in her throat as she saw Lucas watching them steadily, pain etched into his face. Christi gazed back at him over the top of Daisy's silky head, wanting to reach out and hug him too, hating that deep-down sadness about him that not even spending an unexpected day with his children could erase. Because he wanted them for much more than a day!

But she was sure neither of the children noted their father's distracted mood, they were simply loving their day at the beach. The only note of discord came on the drive back to their mother's house.

'Will Mummy and Uncle Julian be home yet?' Robin asked sleepily from the back seat.

Christi's breath was drawn sharply into her lungs, and she glanced anxiously at Lucas, her heart aching at the naked pain in his eyes. She longed to reach out to him, to reassure him with her touch, but if she did that she would be letting him know she had been aware all along of Marsha's plans to remarry. And that would probably hurt him more than telling her about it himself!

So she remained quiet, unmoving, her hands clenched tightly in her lap.

'I should think so, Robin,' his father answered lightly. 'They just had some—arrangements to see to today,' he excused, his grim expression in no way reflected in his casual tone.

'Do you like Uncle Julian, Daddy?' Daisy asked with the innocence of youth, having no idea that the idly put question had caused her father's hands to tighten fiercely on the steering wheel.

'Daisy!' Robin hissed beside his sister.

'Well, I only asked,' Daisy told him defensively, a telltale quiver to her voice at this rebuke from her secretly admired older brother.

'Well, you shouldn't have done,' Robin continued to chastise. 'Don't you know——'

'Hey, come on, kids,' Lucas chided lightly. 'Let's not have an argument about this, all right? I don't really know Uncle Julian, Daisy,' he gently answered her question. 'So I don't know whether or not I like him. I think the important thing is, do you and Robin like him?'

Christi turned away to look out of the side windows, blinking back the tears that threatened to fall. This was only the start for Lucas; it could only get worse as the other man became a permanent fixture in his children's lives.

'He's all right,' Robin dismissed moodily. 'At least he doesn't talk to me as if I'm a baby.'

'And he sometimes reads me my bedtime story,' Daisy added with satisfaction.

This time Christi couldn't prevent it, the action was purely instinctive; she reached blindly for Lucas's hand, the tears falling unashamedly down her cheeks now.

But her vision cleared just as Lucas's hand clasped hers, naked agony in Lucas's eyes as he briefly met her gaze.

Daisy had only been just over a year old when her parents' marriage had broken up, had grown up with the knowledge that as far as she was concerned her mummy and daddy had always lived apart; she would have the least trouble adapting to another man in her mother's life. Whereas Robin had been a little older, two and a half, and still remembered the joy of being a real family, which made him slightly resent the intrusion of another man in his father's place. But he wasn't openly antagonistic towards Julian Holland as a stepfather, which meant he, too, would adapt, in time.

Lucas was the one who would never be able to accept the other man's usurpation of his place in his children's lives.

'That's nice,' Lucas answered his daughter gruffly.

'Although he doesn't do it as well as you do, Daddy,' Daisy assured him guilelessly.

Lucas briefly squeezed Christi's hand, as if thanking her for her support, before returning his own hand back to the steering wheel. 'Give him a chance, poppet,' he told his daughter lightly. 'Uncle Julian isn't quite used to being around little children yet; he'll learn.'

'That's what I said—ouch!' Daisy let out a yell as her brother obviously meted out retribution for her thoughtlessness. 'That hurt,' she said tearfully.

'Robin!' Lucas reproved sternly.

'Sorry,' his son muttered moodily. 'But sometimes Daisy can be such a——'

'That will be enough, Robin,' his father told him firmly. 'I—Uncle Julian is going to be in your lives from now on, so you might as well accept that.'

'But don't you care that—that——'

'Of course I care, Robin.' Lucas's voice was harsher than he would have wished, Christi knew, for the subject was one that had to be handled with extreme delicacy. 'But we have no choice but to accept that your mother loves Uncle Julian, that she wants him in her life. And consequently that means he's in your lives, too.' His tone had gentled.

'I'll always be your daddy, you'll always be able to come to me if you have a problem.'

'Couldn't we come and live with you?' Robin asked petulantly.

Christi stopped breathing altogether. This was far from the perfect place for a father and his children to be having this conversation, but unfortunately Lucas hadn't been able to choose the time and place, but had to answer his children's uncertainties as they came up. Nevertheless, Christi felt as if she were intruding on something that was just too private to be witnessed by what amounted to an outsider. She wished she could just disappear into the night, trying to make herself as inconspicuous as possible.

A nerve pulsed in Lucas's cheek. 'And what would Mummy do then?' he pointed out gently. 'She loves you very much, you know.'

'I know,' Robin accepted carelessly. 'But she has Uncle Julian now, and you don't have anyone.'

There was no arguing with logic like that, and Christi wondered what Lucas's answer would be.

'I have my friends, Robin,' he told his son softly.

'Like Aunty Christi?' Daisy put in brightly.

'Like Aunty Christi,' Lucas nodded abruptly.

'But she doesn't live with you ... Does she ...?' Robin frowned his uncertainty.

'You know she doesn't,' his father reproved.

'But she's at your apartment a lot,' Daisy chimed in pertly.

'That's the way friends are, Daisy,' Lucas told her gently.

'Uncle Julian is going to live with us,' Daisy frowned.

'That's because he and your mother love each other,' Lucas said harshly.

'Don't you love Aunty Christi?' His daughter looked puzzled.

'Of course I love Aunty Christi,' Lucas replied patiently. 'I told you, we're friends, and friends care about each other.'

'But——'

'Stop being silly, Daisy,' her brother rebuked scoffingly. 'Heather is my friend, but I'm not going to *marry* her!' His tone left no doubt as to what he thought of *that* idea concerning his schoolfriend!

'I'm *not* silly,' Daisy protested rebelliously. 'You're the one that's silly. You——'

'I said no arguments, children,' Lucas put in softly. 'We're almost home, and we don't want your mother to think you haven't enjoyed your day at the beach, do we?' he lightly chided.

Christi had no doubt that the idea would please Marsha immensely! The other woman made her so angry, having no compunction in changing Lucas's plans to be with his children whenever it suited her, but quite willing to use him as the willing babysitter he obviously was whenever it fell in with *her* plans.

It was now obvious that Marsha had only let him have the children today so that she could spend time with Julian Holland. It was also obvious that, although the other man was still something of an unknown quantity to Daisy and Robin, they already liked him. Lucas was having to walk a very thin line between his dislike of the idea of the children having a stepfather and not letting the children know of his feelings. And it obviously wasn't easy for him to do.

Marsha Kingsley's house was ablaze with lights as the car turned into the driveway, the children jumping up and down on their seat at the thought of telling their mother all about the lovely day they had had, their earlier disquiet forgotten for the moment.

Lucas had come to the house alone to pick up the children this morning, returning for Christi, and it hadn't occurred to her until this moment that she might actually have to see Marsha and her fiancé when they took the children home.

She hesitated in her seat as Lucas helped the children out of the back.

Lucas bent down to talk to her. 'Coming inside?'

She grimaced. 'I think I'll just wait out here.' She shook her head, not at all eager for another encounter with Marsha Kingsley.

Lucas nodded, the children having already run up to the house to ring the doorbell. 'I can't say I'm exactly looking forward to this myself,' he acknowledged grimly.

There was a pale green BMW parked in the driveway next to Marsha's grey Mercedes, and it didn't take much intelligence to realise the second car must belong to Julian Holland.

Christi made her decision quickly and unhesitantly, opening her car door to step out on to the gravel driveway. 'I think I will come in, after all,' she told Lucas lightly.

He gave her a derisive look as she walked around the car to his side. 'I'm not looking forward to it,' he drawled. 'But I *can* handle it.'

Christi gave a careless shrug. 'I don't really feel like sitting out here in the car.'

Lucas squeezed her arm as he took hold of her elbow to walk beside her up to the door that now stood open, Marsha reflected in the light. 'Thanks,' he murmured before they came into earshot of the other woman.

'Lucas,' Marsha drawled, her sharp hazel gaze turning to Christi. 'And little Christi,' she greeted mockingly. 'Did you enjoy your day at the beach, dear?' she taunted as she held the door open wider for them to enter.

She felt Lucas's fingers tighten on her arm at the deliberate challenge, but her own expression remained impassively calm. 'Of course, you're a little old to enjoy such pleasant pastimes, aren't you?' she returned sweetly.

Marsha's mouth twisted. 'Let's just say I prefer my—amusements, to be a little more mature than days at the beach,' she drawled.

Christi smiled confidently, her arm possessively through the crook of Lucas's; this woman had made her turn tail and run once, she wouldn't succeed in doing it again. 'Oh, I enjoy those sort of amusements, too, at the right time,' she taunted huskily.

Marsha's gaze narrowed on the way Christi and Lucas stood so close together. 'I hope you kept this—relationship from the children?' she snapped.

'Oh, you needn't worry, Marsha dear,' Christi answered before Lucas could, patting the other woman's arm reassuringly. 'Robin and Daisy are still as innocent as I—fortunately!—am not.' The statement was a double-edged sword, telling this woman of her confidence in her own femininity, but also warning her that she was completely wise to the deceit she had practised a week ago, and that she wouldn't fall for it a second time.

She could tell by the way Marsha's lips thinned that neither meaning had been lost on her, and her gaze was angry as it once again swept over the two of them. 'I suppose if you *want* to make a fool of yourself, Lucas——'

'I don't believe *Lucas* is the one making a fool of himself,' Christi cut in bravely, her eyes as hard as the sapphires they resembled.

Marsha flushed. 'What the hell do you mean by that?' Her eyes flashed fire.

Christi met her gaze unflinchingly. 'You must admit, it is a little odd for you to be behaving so possessively towards your ex-husband when, as I understand it, you're thinking of being married again quite soon—to someone else!'

The other woman's mouth tightened even more. 'You——'

'Darling, surely you aren't going to keep Lucas— and his friend,' added the short, slightly overweight man, with receding blond hair, who had joined them from the lounge, as he saw Christi standing at Lucas's side, 'standing out here all evening?'

This was Julian Holland? He wasn't at all what Christi had been expecting, and she stared at him in open astonishment.

He wasn't much taller than Marsha's five foot five in her three-inch-heel sandals, for one thing, and was certainly a couple of inches shorter than Christi herself. And, although his looks were quite pleasant—warm brown eyes and a round, friendly face—he wasn't what Christi could call in the least sexy or heart-stoppingly attractive the way Lucas was. Although his suit was obviously an expensive one, it didn't look half as good on him as Lucas did in jeans and a casual shirt, for Julian's stocky build was only slightly concealed by the excellent tailoring.

But he obviously *was* Julian Holland, his arm moving lightly about Marsha's waist as he reached her side, his bulkier appearance making Marsha look tinier than ever.

Lucas was the first to recover. 'Holland.' He held out his hand politely.

Something in Lucas's tone put the other man on his guard, Julian Holland eyeing him warily. 'Kingsley,' he returned slowly.

Lucas nodded tersely. 'If I could just say goodbye to the children?' He turned to Marsha.

Marsha's gaze swept challengingly over Christi before settling on Lucas. 'Don't you want to help me put them to bed, the way you usually do when you bring them home?' she suggested huskily.

His gaze unconsciously turned to Christi before he shook his head. 'I don't think——'

'Please go ahead and help put the children to bed, Lucas,' Christi cut in sharply, knowing he must be longing to spend even that little more time with the children he saw all too infrequently. 'I'm sure Mr Holland and I can amuse ourselves while we wait in the lounge for the two of you.' She gave the other man a brief smile, having chosen her wording carefully, knowing Marsha hadn't missed the implication. She looked outraged by the challenge.

Lucas hesitated. 'If you're sure you don't mind...?'

'Of course I don't,' her smile was warm with feeling as she turned to him, 'and I'm sure the children will love it,' she added indulgently.

While Lucas rounded up the children for their baths, Julian Holland moved to pour Christi a drink, Christi and Marsha eyeing each other speculatively.

A grudging respect slowly entered the other woman's eyes. 'You really did grow up, didn't you?' she mused.

Christi gave an abrupt inclination of her head. 'I really did.'

Marsha glanced at Lucas as he laughingly threw Daisy over his shoulder to carry her out of the room. 'But I wonder if you grew up enough?' she murmured without a second glance, following the man who had once been her husband, and her children, from the room.

Christi let out a shaky breath, sitting down in the nearest chair before she fell down. Marsha might be going to marry the pleasant-faced man who was now handing her the sherry she had requested, but she certainly had no intention of relinquishing her claim on Lucas at the same time!

'Cheers!' Julian Holland held up his glass before taking an obviously welcome swallow of the whisky inside it. 'Have you known—er—Lucas, long?' he enquired casually as he sat down opposite her, obviously awkward with the familiarity after Lucas's terse formality.

'Several years,' she nodded abruptly, feeling a little sorry for him, but also very much aware that he was the reason for Lucas's present unhappiness.

His eyes widened. 'Really? I wouldn't have thought—you don't look old enough—well, isn't that nice!' He gave a bright, meaningless smile.

For a diplomat, this man certainly wasn't very diplomatic! 'Isn't it?' she agreed drily. 'Have you known Marsha very long?' He couldn't have done if he were contemplating marrying her!

He smiled as he thought of the woman he loved. 'A few months.'

'How nice.' She turned away uninterestedly, pretending interest in one of the paintings that hung on the wall. It wasn't this man's fault, and under any other circumstances she would probably have liked him, but she couldn't help but feel angry at

what this man's marriage to Marsha would do to
Lucas.

'Do you like that?' He squinted up at the abstract painting Christi was staring at so fixedly.

How could anyone like green and pink lines on
a canvas? 'No,' she answered with blunt honesty,
sighing as the man opposite her looked uncomfortable. 'Look, I'm sorry, this—this awkward situation isn't your fault, but I don't think either of us
really feels like making polite conversation.'

'No,' he conceded with a weary sigh, relaxing
back in his chair slightly. 'It is a little awkward,
isn't it?'

A little? It was impossible! But if she *had* been
the woman in Lucas's life, as this man believed her
to be, it would have been even more uncomfortable.

God, if she'd really had the right to tell Marsha
what she thought of her, she certainly wouldn't have
hit out at the other woman with veiled innuendoes
about Lucas and herself, she would have left
Marsha in no doubt as to her claim to him and
would have shown Marsha that she could have a
fight on her hands for custody of the children. Instead, she had to stand by and watch Marsha de-
stroy Lucas that little bit more. No wonder Lucas
was incapable of loving another woman after
Marsha! She had taken all he had to give, was *still*
taking what little peace of mind he managed to
attain for himself.

The silence in the room as they waited for the
return of Lucas and Marsha was very uncomfortable, and Christi passed the time by looking at each

of the abstract paintings in turn and trying to vis-
ualise what had sparked off the monstrosities in the
artist's mind in the first place. She had just decided
the one on the far wall was a bloated fish when
Lucas and Marsha came into the room.

Under any other circumstances, their flushed and
dishevelled appearance would have looked highly
suspect, but the damp patches on their clothing told
their own story, although the indulgent smiles they
shared about their children's antics in the bath
caused a painful lurch in Christi's chest.

She stood up jerkily. 'Finished?' Her voice was
unnaturally high, her cheeks flushed.

'I——'

'Cook is just about to serve dinner,' Marsha
lightly interrupted Lucas. 'I'm sure there's enough
for four—if you would care to stay?'

If you would *dare* to stay! Christi read the challenge clearly in her words. The last thing she wanted
was to sit down to dinner with this woman in the
name of civilised behaviour, and yet she knew that
if Lucas chose to accept she would be at his side.

She deliberately kept her expression bland, her
gaze averted, not wanting to influence his decision.

'Thanks for the invitation, Marsha,' Lucas's
hand came to rest lightly against Christi's back, 'but
I'm afraid we've made other arrangements.'

Christi's breath left her in a relieved sigh, and as
she looked up at Lucas she could see the amusement
in his eyes, evidence that she had given herself away
seconds ago. She returned his smile ruefully.

'In that case, don't let us keep you,' Marsha's caustic voice interrupted the moment of shared humour.

Lucas nodded abruptly to Julian Holland as he stood up, his gaze then flickering to Marsha. 'If you need somewhere to park the children again soon, let me know,' he rasped.

'I think all the arrangements for the wedding next month are completed now, thank you,' Marsha returned scornfully. 'You'll receive your invitation in due time, of course,' she added bitchily. 'And you must bring dear Christi.'

Her eyes narrowed on the other woman. 'I wouldn't miss it for anything!'

Marsha gave a mocking smile. '"Always the bridesmaid, never the bride",' she taunted.

Although the barb hit its mark, it wasn't obvious from Christi's relaxed pose at Lucas's side. 'Is that an invitation?' she derided.

'What do you think?' Marsha snapped.

Christi gave her a mocking smile before turning to Julian Holland; the poor man was starting to look a little dazed by this whole encounter now. 'Nice to have met you, Mr Holland. I'm sorry the next time we meet can't be under better circumstances,' she added with sweet sarcasm.

How Lucas managed to get her out of the house without Marsha physically attacking her she couldn't say, but minutes later they were in his car, driving away from the house, and she didn't have a scratch mark on her!

Lucas chuckled at her side. 'I never thought I would see the day that Marsha would be left speechless,' he explained at her frowning look.

'Was that what it was?' she sighed, some of the tension starting to leave her. 'I thought she was just trying to prevent Julian Holland from seeing her true nature!'

Lucas instantly sobered, and Christi could have kicked herself for her lack of tact. 'You'll have gathered by now that the two of them are getting married,' he bit out abruptly.

How could she help but know? 'Yes,' she sighed.

'He wasn't quite what I was expecting—hell, I don't know what I was expecting!' Lucas shook his head. 'The kids seem to like him, don't you think?' He glanced at her before his attention returned to the road in front of them.

'They like you better,' Christi rasped.

'And the thought of any other man but me in their life breaks me up, but——' He broke off abruptly, sighing heavily. 'We all had a good day together today, didn't we?' he lightly changed the subject.

'Very good,' she agreed huskily. 'Robin and Daisy are lovely children.'

'Yes,' he said heavily. 'Yes, they are.'

There didn't seem to be anything else to say on the subject; Lucas was lost in his own thoughts as they drove back towards town, and Christi didn't want to intrude on those thoughts, knowing he needed this time to himself.

Finally he gave a deep sigh, shaking off his oppressive mood. 'Shall we go home and change first before going out to dinner, or do you want to find somewhere that will accept us dressed like this?' He looked down ruefully at the denims they both wore, he with an open-necked shirt, Christi with a pale blue blouse.

She was surprised to learn that he had meant it about the two of them having dinner together, had thought it had just been a way to get away from Marsha's invitation. After all, it was a Saturday night, and Lucas usually had a date on a Saturday night.

'No Michelle tonight?' she enquired lightly.

He smiled teasingly. 'I would hardly be asking you to go out to dinner with me if there were.'

Now, there was a logic she couldn't argue with—and didn't want to! She was glad the other woman at last seemed to have faded from his life. 'I could always get us something at my apartment,' she offered. 'I feel a little too salty and sandy still to go straight out,' she explained as he hesitated. 'And it will be a little late to go anywhere by the time we've both showered and changed.'

'Asking you to cook dinner doesn't seem very fair after you've helped me entertain the children all day,' he frowned.

She should have known the dinner invitation was a thank you for going out with them today! 'I really don't mind,' she said a little flatly.

'What if I cook dinner, instead?' he suggested lightly, giving her a brief grin. 'You seem just as sleepy from your day by the sea as the children were!'

Just what she needed, to be classed with a six- and seven-year-old! 'I'm fine,' she reassured him sharply. 'More than capable of cooking us some dinner.'

'OK,' Lucas accepted shruggingly.

Christi hurried into her own apartment once they got back, anxious to wash the salt and sand from her body now, absently acknowledging Lucas's comment of 'see you soon'.

If nothing else, she needed these few minutes alone to put the meeting with Marsha from her mind. The other woman was a possessive bitch who kept Lucas tied to her by using their children, and who had made it obvious she didn't intend relinquishing that hold even once she had remarried, by reminding him all too forcefully of his relationship with her through his children if he should ever start to think of a life of his own, separate from theirs. Lucas would *never* give up his relationship with his children, but surely he didn't have to pay for the rest of his life for the mistake of his marriage to their mother, a marriage that Marsha herself had chosen to end? It just didn't seem fair!

She must have spent longer under the shower than she had realised, just letting the steaming hot water beat down on her as *she* inwardly steamed at the injustice of the emotional blackmail Marsha felt no hesitation in using to keep Lucas running to her side, because she could hear the doorbell ringing now. Realising it must be Lucas, arriving for the dinner she had promised to cook him, she hastily switched off the shower tap, opening the door to wrap the towel around her wet hair in the process of stepping from the shower when a movement near the door caught her eye.

She froze in the action of picking up the second towel she had laid out to dry herself with, her startled gaze fixed on Lucas's suddenly pale face as he stood in the bathroom doorway.

'I used my key to get in.' He explained his presence gruffly. 'I thought you might have fallen and hurt yourself, or—God...' he breathed shakily, his dark gaze held mesmerised by her nakedness.

Christi knew she should pick up the towel from the side of the bath, that she should wrap it around herself, should laugh off this awkward situation. But she didn't want to do any of those things; she wanted to lose herself in the heated admiration she could see in Lucas's eyes, unconsciously standing more proudly, her breasts thrusting pertly forward, her waist slender and flat, her thighs silkily inviting.

Lucas swallowed hard, breathing raggedly. 'I think I should wait for you in the lounge,' he murmured huskily, although he made no effort to leave the confines of the steamily hot room.

Christi moved slowly forward, her breathing shallow. 'Lucas,' she said softly, holding his gaze with hers.

He stood rigidly still. 'I should go...'

But he didn't. He swayed slightly as she came to stand in front of him, but it was his only movement.

Christi put her arms up about his neck, absently noting how white her skin looked against the black shirt he wore with a clean pair of denims, her breath catching in her throat as the soft material of his shirt became a caress against her breasts.

Lucas moved as if in a daze, his arms slowly encircling her, reaching up to pull the towel from her hair.

Until that moment Christi had forgotten the towel wrapped about her wet hair, and shivered slightly as the cold tendrils fell on her heated shoulders. And then Lucas was threading his fingers through the silky dampness to cup her head for the descent of his lips, and fire was the only thing she was aware of.

There was no gentleness, only fierce demand, his mouth moving expertly against hers, tasting her like a man who had been starving in a desert.

She entwined her arms more tightly about his neck, glad of her height as their thighs met in abrasive demand, Lucas hard against her.

He wanted her! If she had ever doubted it before, she knew it for certain now, his body's involuntary reaction something he couldn't hide.

His hands were like fire against her, and she shuddered with emotions too long suppressed as one of those hands closed over the tautness of her breast, easing some of the aching heat there as his thumb-pad stroked the hardened tip.

'I want you,' he groaned against the silky length of her throat. 'Dear God, I want you so badly!'

Nerves pulsed and leapt as his mouth caressed her shoulders, his tongue searching out the creamy hollows of her throat.

Her whole body tingled with need, her back arching as his mouth finally took her breast, suckling against the fiery nub in a slow rhythm that made her legs tremble and quake.

Christi held him to her, wanting more, groaning her satisfaction as his teeth nibbled against her with pleasure-pain.

Liquid fire met him between her thighs as he caressed her there, groaning low in his throat at this evidence of her readiness for him.

She wouldn't have cared if Lucas had lain her down on the bathroom floor and taken her there, so great was her need for him, but Lucas had other ideas. He swung her up into his arms to carry her into her bedroom, laying her down gently on the bed, before standing over her.

Christi groaned at the indecision in his face. 'Don't go, Lucas.' She held out her arms to him, her expression pleading. 'Stay, and make love to me.' She almost sobbed with her need.

As he still hesitated, his face racked by indecision, Christi came up on her knees on the bed, holding his gaze as she began to unbutton his shirt, running shaking hands over the hardness of his flesh before slipping the shirt from his body completely.

His chest was covered with fine dark hair that disappeared in a V beneath the material of his jeans, and Christi's questing lips followed the path of that silky hair, gazing up at him with pleading eyes as her fingers moved to the fastening of his denims.

Lucas swallowed convulsively, one of his hands moving to cover both of hers. 'Christi, we can't——'

'We can,' she insisted firmly. 'Let me, Lucas,' she groaned, looking at him with dark blue eyes.

He gave a low moan, his eyes slowly closing as his hand fell away from hers, although both his hands moved into clenched fists as Christi slid the denims from his body.

She had seen him only that afternoon in bathing trunks, had thought then he was the most beautiful man she had ever seen. But naked he was even more so, like a gold and bronze sculpture come to life, every part of him beautifully smooth and firmly muscled.

He stood perfectly still as her searching hands and lips learned every inch of him, his increased ragged breathing and his tensed muscles the only outward evidence that he was fast losing control.

Suddenly he couldn't stand any more; his hands gripped her arms tightly as he stopped her caresses, pushing her down on the bed before covering her body with his, his mouth fiercely possessing hers as his tongue fought a silent duel with hers.

Christi felt like sobbing with the sheer beauty of the moment, giving herself up completely to the wild sensations coursing through her body as Lucas caressed her as intimately as she had him only seconds earlier, gasping as he sought her out in a way she hadn't dared to with him, writhing on the bed with heated abandon as that liquid fire flooded her whole body.

'Now, Lucas,' she choked her desperation. 'Lucas, it has to be now!'

The soft lamp-glow made his eyes look almost blue as he looked down at her searchingly. 'Did you really mean it—about those other men?' His voice was gruff.

'Mean it?' she echoed wildly, not understanding what he meant. And then, as his gaze roamed regretfully over her body, she knew. 'It isn't going to make any difference, Lucas?' she cried brokenly. 'You aren't going to be noble, are you?' She shook her head in silent denial.

He gave a self-derisive snort. 'I stopped being noble with you the moment I walked into your bathroom and found you naked. But I have to know, Christi.' His fingertips ran caressingly down one cheek. 'I don't want to hurt you.''

She swallowed hard. 'I've never wanted anyone else but you, Lucas. Does that answer your question?' She was completely vulnerable as she gazed up at him.

'Yes,' he breathed softly. 'Dear God, Christi,' he groaned suddenly. 'I wish I *could* stop this.' He grimaced as if in pain. 'But it's too late for that, far too late!' He shook his head weakly.

'I love you, Lucas.' She smoothed the frown from between his eyes. 'I've always loved you.'

'It doesn't help—I have no right—but I need— I *can't* fight that need any more!' He shook his head self-disgustedly, his mouth savagely claiming hers even as his thighs surged against her, seeking entrance, surging into her as he found his way blocked by that gossamer barrier, her cry of pain lost, and then forgotten, as she moved with him instinctively.

Christi felt complete for the first time in her life, and as that aching fire grew and grew in her body she knew there was even more, feeling herself rising higher and higher, seeking, searching——

'Marry me, Christi,' Lucas groaned heatedly, his body a silky caress against hers. 'Marry me!'

'Yes! Oh God, yes!' Sensations unlike any she had ever known racked her body, taking it in wave after wave of blissful pleasure, aware of the deep surge of Lucas's body as he too reached the peak of fulfilment, sobbing quietly in his arms as the beauty of their shared passion washed over her.

Long after Lucas had fallen into a deep sleep, neither of them interested in the dinner that had once seemed so appealing, Christi lay awake, her heart once again feeling as if it were breaking.

She had wanted Lucas's loving, had begged for it, but he hadn't spoken of loving her, had only allowed his body to do that, while his thoughts had remained detached from what he was doing.

She had watched him with the children today, knew the torment he was going through at the thought of some other man bringing them up, knew that he had been driven by desperation tonight, had been fighting for the right to have custody to his children in the only way that now seemed open to him: if he were married himself, he would have more to offer his children than ever before.

And what better choice for a wife than the young woman he had always known was in love with him? He had said he 'had no right', but that he 'needed', and in that moment Christi had known *why* he needed her.

But it hadn't mattered. Not then, and not now. Her heart was breaking at the way Lucas had finally become hers, but she knew he had no other choice, that at least they could be friends and lovers even if Lucas couldn't offer her any more than that. He *had* to have a wife if he were to stand any chance of getting custody of Robin and Daisy, and with Marsha's wedding next month he didn't have any time to waste.

Christi looked down at him with loving eyes as he lay against her breast. Long dark lashes fanned out across his cheeks, giving him a boyish appeal, leaving him completely vulnerable.

Her arms tightened about him. She didn't care how or why he was hers, only that he was.

And she was going to marry him.

CHAPTER SEVEN

'WHAT do you mean, you're getting married next week?' Dizzy blustered down the telephone line.

Christi smiled as she envisaged her friend's surprise: the green eyes wide with shock, her mouth open with disbelief.

These Sunday evening telephone calls between the two friends had been a ritual for as long as Christi could remember, carried on even after Dizzy's marriage to Christi's uncle, and although Christi didn't usually have anything too dramatic to report, today was different. Today she had to tell Dizzy and Zach that she intended marrying Lucas, very soon.

'Exactly what I said,' she mused. 'I hope you and Zach can make it before you have to leave for the States.'

'Zach's doing the work here for the moment,' Dizzy dismissed vaguely. 'You know how cautious he can be.'

'Except when he married you,' Christi chuckled. 'A three-day courtship had to take him a little by surprise!'

'No more than yours is going to!' Dizzy sounded as if she were frowning. 'I don't understand it, last week you said they were all nice, but none of them were special. Last week you were so angry with Dick

129

and Barry—and me!—because you found out they
were trying to use you to get to your uncle...
David!' she pounced. 'It has to be David,' she said
wonderingly.

Christi couldn't blame her friend for jumping to
that conclusion. She herself was still a little dazed
that *Lucas* was to be her husband next week!

Not that he hadn't given her the chance to change
her mind about accepting his proposal. His desperation of Saturday night seemed to have worn
off by this morning; he'd assured her that the
chances of her being pregnant from that one night
were unlikely, and that if she would like to recon-
sider her decision he would understand. Considering all that he had to lose if she should decide not
to marry him, she had only loved him all the more
for his unselfishness. But she loved him, even if his
only reason for wanting to marry her was his
children, and to be his wife this way was better than
not being his wife at all.

'No, it isn't David,' she told her friend drily.

'Not David? But—Lucas,' Dizzy said with satisfaction. 'He finally realised that he loves you!'

'What?' Now it was Christi's turn to be amazed.
How in the world had Dizzy guessed that Christi
was in love with Lucas?

'It is him, isn't it?' her friend persisted eagerly.

'Well, yes... But——'

'How did I know?' Dizzy finished excitedly.
'How did you know I was in love with your uncle
when I was still fighting the idea myself?' she dismissed. 'We've always been so close, Christi, how

could I not know? I took one look at the two of you together at my wedding and knew he was the reason no other man has ever meant anything serious to you. All those years he had been your next-door neighbour and I'd never guessed a thing, but as soon as I saw you together, I knew.'

'OK, Sherlock,' Christi drawled, 'what gave me away?'

'The love in your eyes every time you looked at him,' her friend said softly.

She swallowed hard. 'Oh—that,' she mumbled.

'And now the two of you are finally going to be married,' Dizzy cried gleefully. 'My effort at long-distance matchmaking paid off, then?'

'What do you——? Dick, Barry and David were supposed to make Lucas jealous?' she realised slowly.

'It worked, didn't it?' her friend gloated. 'Although, what Zach's going to say about the wedding being next week, I don't know,' she added worriedly.

Christi was still dazed by Dizzy's instinctive knowledge of the love for Lucas she had tried for so long to hide from everyone. 'What if your plan had gone wrong?' she protested weakly.

'And you had actually fallen in love with Dick, Barry, or David?' Dizzy said cheerfully. 'Well, that wouldn't have been so bad, would it? They're all very nice men, although I have to admit David is my favourite,' she added fondly.

'Mine, too,' Christi acknowledged softly. 'But, Dizzy——'

'Oh, love, you had tried everything else to get Lucas to see you as a woman,' Dizzy dismissed. 'I just had this feeling you were getting to the "it's now or never" stage.'

She should have realised Dizzy knew her too well! 'If you think back, I had also tried the jealousy bit before,' she said drily.

'Not with men of Lucas's own age and experience,' her friend returned confidently. 'That was sure to get him to sit up and take notice. Oh, love, I'm so glad for you,' she sighed happily.

'And *I* should be angry with you.' Christi tried to sound indignant.

'But you aren't, are you?' Dizzy chuckled.

How could she be, when possibly Dizzy's matchmaking *had* helped to show Lucas she was a grown woman, to prove to him that *other* men considered her mature enough to take on the responsibility of a relationship? He was marrying her, wasn't he? So he must finally see her as all grown up. At least, grown up enough to become stepmother to the two children he wanted back with him so desperately.

'No,' she admitted drily. 'I'm not angry with you at all.'

'I'll get Zach so that you can discuss the wedding with him,' Dizzy told her briskly.

'Coward!' Christi softly taunted.

'Guilty as charged,' Dizzy laughed before going off in search of her husband.

Knowing how Dizzy could twist her husband around her little finger, Christi knew her friend would have done her best to persuade Zach around to the idea of her marriage to Lucas before he even came on the telephone, especially as it now turned out to have been Dizzy's idea in the first place!

However, her best friend couldn't possibly have guessed at the impossible position Lucas found himself in that necessitated him having a wife.

She was proved right about Dizzy's influence with Zach, for her uncle gave his approval unhesitantly. Apparently, he had liked Lucas when he'd met him at the wedding last year and, as Zach wryly claimed, 'We older men make the best husbands.' A second later, he muttered, 'Ouch!' as Dizzy obviously hit him for his facetiousness.

Christi was chuckling softly to herself as she came off the telephone, her smile fading as the doorbell rang and Henry set up the excited yapping that told her it was Lucas at the door.

She hadn't seen him since they had had breakfast together earlier, Lucas claiming he had some work to do. Christi was sure the work had just been an excuse, that Lucas himself needed time to come to terms with the idea of becoming a husband again. Although surely the pill must be sweeter to swallow when it also meant he stood a chance of becoming full-time father to Robin and Daisy again!

Oh God, bitterness wasn't going to make a success of this relationship that was already a fact because of all the wrong reasons; she had made her decision with her eyes wide open, she didn't have room for doubts now.

'Lucas,' she greeted him warmly as she threw open the door, the shadows dispelled from all but the depths of her eyes.

He hesitated only fractionally before kissing her lightly on the mouth, but it was enough to be noticeable when Christi was already feeling so sensitive.

'I thought we would go out for dinner,' he suggested abruptly.

She could see that, his appearance in the dark evening suit taking her breath away. She didn't want to go out anywhere, she just wanted Lucas to take her in his arms and reassure her, in the only way in which they seemed to be close now, that everything would be all right, that he did care for her.

But the distant expression in his eyes, and the grim set to his mouth, didn't encourage such intimacies. The erotically beautiful man of the night before was far removed from this harsh-faced stranger.

'Just give me a few minutes to change,' she nodded lightly.

'Fine.' He sat down in an armchair, opening up the newspaper that had been delivered that day, immediately lost behind the voluminous pages.

Christi watched him woefully for several seconds before hastily leaving the room. Lucas didn't seem able to even look at her now!

She was shaking badly by the time she reached her bedroom, burying her face in Josephine's fur as the cat stood on her dressing-table to rub against her concernedly. 'I think he actually hates me,

Josie,' she wailed brokenly, the haughty animal not in the least offended by this shortened version of her name, butting her gently with her regal head.

No, he didn't hate *her*, she reasoned as the pain lessened, Lucas just hated the situation Marsha's remarriage had put them both in. But Christi loved him, would always love him, and it didn't really matter *why* he was marrying her, as long as he did.

All trace of tears had been deftly removed when she rejoined Lucas in the lounge a few minutes later, the off-the-shoulder white dress having a gypsy style to it, her hair secured to one side to fall in loose curls over one of those bare shoulders, her make-up suitably dramatic, hiding evidence of her earlier distress. She felt good, and she knew she looked good.

Lucas put the newspaper down slowly, the darkening of his eyes the only outward sign of his approval of her appearance as he stood up to briskly drape her jacket over her shoulders.

But that involuntary reaction was enough for Christi, and she shot him a provocative smile over one shoulder as his hands lingered caressingly against her.

His hands were abruptly removed as he turned away. 'With you dressed like this, I feel we should do more than just go out to dinner,' he rasped.

If their engagement were a normal one, she would have moved into his arms and told him she didn't want to go out at all, that she would much rather stay here, in his arms, making love as passionately as they had last night.

But they weren't like any normally engaged couple, and so she just smiled brightly. 'Dinner sounds just fine,' she assured him.

He nodded distantly, his hand politely on her elbow as they left her apartment to go down to his waiting car.

This wasn't the Lucas she was used to, the Lucas she could tell anything to, and know he would either sympathise or offer advice that wasn't intrusive.

She could have wept for the friendship they had sacrificed, but Lucas had to think it was worth it to have his children back with him. She pushed from her mind thoughts of what would happen to her and Lucas if he should lose the battle for custody of his children...

She smiled a little wanly at Simon as he saw them to their table, hoping he wouldn't connect her with the woman who had telephoned that night to arrange a table for Mr Kingsley, only to find Lucas was already taking Marsha out to dinner! She knew Simon to be a man of quick intelligence, his watchful gaze not missing a movement in 'his' restaurant, and if he had recognised her voice that night he remained silent now.

Lucas's tension didn't relent as the meal progressed, and conversation was an uphill battle Christi felt she was fast losing. Ordinarily, silence between them would have been companionable, but now Christi was afraid that if she left a lull in the conversation Lucas might take it to voice the doubts he seemed to be having about them, and seemed to be having more with each passing minute.

She couldn't even remember the meal she ate, and considering the exquisiteness of the menu served there that was evidence of her disturbed peace of mind!

'—Dizzy and Zach about the wedding...' Her voice trailed off lamely as she realised exactly what she had been babbling, her stricken gaze raised to Lucas's sudden stillness. She hadn't meant to mention that telephone call, hadn't meant to talk of their marriage *at all*!

Lucas sat back, his hands resting lightly on the table's edge. 'Oh?'

She swallowed hard. 'I wanted to make sure they didn't go off to America before I'd had a chance to tell them,' she explained with a grimace, having told Lucas over breakfast that morning of Zach's dual careers. He had been a little surprised, but obviously had other things on his mind. Now he was all too intent on what she was saying.

'I intended going up to see your uncle tomorrow,' Lucas bit out abruptly.

Her eyes widened. 'You never said...'

He shrugged. 'I haven't seen you all day to tell you anything.'

'No, but—I'm sorry if I ruined your plans,' she frowned. 'I thought I was just getting one obstacle out of the way,' she grimaced.

His eyes narrowed. 'And is it?' he drawled slowly.

She longed to tell him of the teasing comment her uncle had made about 'older men', but Lucas just wasn't approachable enough just now. 'Zach intends staying in England to write the screenplay,' she answered hollowly. 'So he and Dizzy will be in England for several more months yet.'

'How about next week?' Lucas grated.

She moved her shoulders shruggingly. 'Next week, too.'

'I meant,' he bit out slowly, 'how did your uncle feel about us being married next week?'

She gave a wan smile. 'He seemed to think that after knowing each other for four years it was about time!'

Lucas gave an impatient sigh. 'It seems to me he could show a little more concern for your welfare!' He looked angry.

'Why?' Christi looked at him curiously. 'Are you going to beat me? Keep me barefoot and pregnant for the next ten years?' Her eyes gleamed mischievously.

There was no answering smile in Lucas's expression. 'Of course not,' he rasped harshly. 'But I hope I would show a little bit more interest in the man Daisy chose to marry.'

Daisy. And Robin. The reason he was marrying her in the first place.

She gave a deep sigh. 'I think I've spoken of you enough over the years for my uncle to realise you're a kind and wonderful man, that you'll be good to me, c-care for me,' she completed briskly, not knowing if that last were true any more. 'And your business reputation is something he doesn't need to be told about,' she dismissed abruptly. 'What else does he need to know about the man I'm going to marry?' *That he loved her,* but that was something she couldn't assure Zach!

'So he's agreeable to the wedding being next week?' Lucas snapped.

'Of course,' she nodded.

Lucas lapsed into silence again, nodding for the bill, frowning darkly as he waited for it to be brought to the table.

'I was invited to a party tonight.' He spoke harshly once they had left the restaurant. 'I wasn't going to go, but—well, we might as well put in an appearance,' he shrugged.

Was he testing her? Had he decided that not just any wife would do, that she would have to fit in with his friends and life-style, too? She couldn't think of any other reason why he should suddenly decide the party seemed like a good idea, after all; he hadn't even mentioned it to her until now.

Accepting that he didn't return her love was one thing, understanding his need to have Daisy and Robin with him was another, but she wouldn't be put on trial as to her abilities to be a suitable wife for him!

'I'm not sure I——'

'Have a little patience, Christi!' Lucas gave a rueful grimace. 'I'm a little out of practice with considering another person's wishes. Would you *like* to go on to a party with me?'

Even this slight softening in his harshly remote mood was enough to make her feel like crying! 'I'd love to go to a party with you.' She gave a shaky smile.

She had been to dozens of other parties just like this one turned out to be, and even knew several of the people there, although she could tell she and Lucas were the centre of some attention for attending this party together.

'I know actresses like to "make an entrance", but this is ridiculous!' murmured a conspiratorial voice at her side.

Christi turned eagerly to greet David Kendrick, kissing his cheek warmly, having felt a little conspicuous standing on her own while Lucas went to the bar to get them both another drink.

'Do that again,' David invited wolfishly, his eyes gleaming with laughter.

She gave a husky laugh as she saw several people were looking their way. 'I don't think I'd better,' she said ruefully.

David glanced about them too, grimacing. 'Maybe not,' he drawled, suddenly very serious. 'Am I allowed to ask what you're doing here with Lucas?' He frowned his puzzlement.

'Enjoying the party?' she shrugged.

'Besides that,' he dismissed thoughtfully. 'As far as I know, you've never been to one of these parties with him before.'

Lucas was standing across the room, engaged in conversation with another man now, although she knew he was aware of her own conversation with David, having seen him glance in their direction a few seconds ago, only to turn away again uninterestedly.

She turned to give David a bright smile. 'That's right, I haven't.'

'Christi——'

'Would you like to be among the first to congratulate us—me?' she continued lightly. 'Lucas and I are to be married next week.'

Instead of answering her, David looked at her searchingly, concern in the dark blue eyes. 'Why?' he finally asked.

She laughed softly, keeping the despair firmly at bay. 'Why do people usually get married?' she derided.

'Because they love each other,' he dismissed. 'Now, tell me, why are you and Lucas getting married?'

'Really, David——'

'Christi,' he put his hand on her arm, squeezing lightly, 'it's too sudden to just be a coincidence so soon after I told you about Marsha remarrying.'

Her head went back proudly. 'I happen to love Lucas very much.'

He nodded. 'And it's obvious from the way he was behaving the other night that he feels he has a proprietorial claim on you, too, but that isn't reason enough for him to marry you.'

Christi drew in a ragged breath. 'We're getting married because it's what we want to do.' She *couldn't* lie and say that Lucas returned her love.

'And you're saying Marsha's plans to remarry have nothing to do with it, hmm?' David frowned.

'I'm saying——' She breathed heavily. 'I'm saying that this is really none of your business, David,' she told him regretfully.

He nodded without rancour. 'I suppose not. I just—— Are you sure this is what you really want to do, Christi?' he prompted gently.

She gave a choked groan. 'I——'

'Kendrick.' Lucas's hard drawl cut in on the conversation as he moved to stand at Christi's side. 'I didn't see you here earlier.' His eyes were narrowed on David as he handed Christi her drink.

'I only arrived a few minutes ago,' David dismissed lightly. 'I hear congratulations are in order?' He held out his hand.

Christi watched as the two men warily shook hands, eyeing each other critically, almost as if they were sizing each other up for a fight.

Lucas touched her for the first time since driving to the restaurant earlier this evening, his arm lightly about her waist. 'To me, certainly,' he rasped. 'To Christi, I'm not so sure,' he shrugged.

'Hm.' David eyed him mockingly. 'You certainly aren't my type, but I believe women find you fascinating,' he derided.

Christi gave him a grateful smile for lightening the conversation, looking up at Lucas with loving eyes. 'I'm certainly happy with my choice.' She put her hand possessively on his chest.

'And that's the important thing,' David said lightly, before Lucas could make any comment. 'And now, if the two of you will excuse me, I've ignored my date long enough.' He smiled wolfishly at the beautiful blonde woman watching him across the room. 'Are your beautiful fiancée and I still allowed to have lunch together tomorrow as we'd arranged?' he paused to ask Lucas, as if in afterthought.

But Christi knew that it wasn't an afterthought at all, that David was determined to talk to her again about her plans to marry Lucas. And it wasn't too difficult to guess why! In truth, she had forgotten all about her agreement to have lunch with David tomorrow, but after tonight she had no doubt what their main topic of conversation was going to be!

Lucas was standing stiffly at her side. 'Christi is perfectly at liberty to spend time with whom she chooses,' he grated abruptly.

David quirked a mocking eyebrow. 'You didn't give that impression the other evening,' he mocked. 'Still,' he added lightly as Lucas's expression darkened ominously. 'I'm glad if my intrusion on the situation made you realise you're in love with Christi, after all. See you tomorrow, Christi,' he added firmly before strolling across the room to join the beautiful blonde.

Christi chanced a glance at Lucas, instantly wishing she hadn't; his face looked as if it were carved from granite, his eyes narrowed to silver slits.

'If you would rather I didn't have lunch with David——'

'I told you both, you can spend time with whom you want to,' Lucas interrupted harshly. 'Our marriage isn't going to be a prison, Christi,' he said firmly. 'I don't expect you to give up your friends just because you're married to me.'

As he wouldn't give up his 'friends'? She couldn't survive a marriage like that! 'Friends, no,' she conceded lightly. 'But surely anything else?' she tried to tease, although the subject was much too important to her to take lightly. But wouldn't Lucas, a man who had become used to the freedom of bachelorhood, and the relationships that went along with that freedom, find it difficult to suddenly find himself with just one woman in his life again?

He looked at her steadily. 'I thought you said nothing like that happened between you and Kendrick?' he rasped.

Her cheeks coloured warmly. 'You know that it didn't. I meant—well, I meant *you*.' She frowned.

Lucas's expression darkened even more. 'Just what the hell are you implying?'

Christi glanced about them awkwardly, very conscious of the party going on around them. 'Perhaps it would be better if we left now,' she suggested awkwardly. 'It's late, and I start work on the commercials tomorrow.'

'We'll leave, Christi,' he nodded tersely. 'But this conversation is far from over,' he warned grimly.

She was conscious of David's concerned gaze on her as she stood at Lucas's side making their farewells to their host and hostess. She deliberately refused to meet that gaze, aware that things were tense enough between Lucas and herself without him finding her and David relaying silent messages to each other across the room!

Christi sat tensely at Lucas's side on the drive home, wondering just when he was going to resume that 'conversation' that had so angered him. But could she be blamed for having her doubts? He had never once said he loved her, and his manner hadn't exactly been loverlike towards her today!

'This is ridiculous, Lucas,' she attacked impatiently once they reached her apartment.

'I couldn't agree more,' he said harshly, very dark and forbidding. And, when he had been one of her best friends until yesterday, it was a little difficult to take! 'I realise marriage to me is a big step for you to take, but after Marsha ended *our* marriage because she decided it was too restrictive, do you honestly think I would do the same thing to someone else?'

One of those statements stood out more than the others: marriage to him was a big step for her to take. Because they both knew he was using that marriage in order to try and get his children into his custody, and that once he had them back with him she would be expected to become their stepmother.

'I *like* being married, Christi,' he added gruffly. 'I like sharing breakfast with the same woman every morning, rather than some woman I can hardly remember the name of, I like coming home to that same woman in the evenings, having dinner with her, sleeping with her. I even like the arguments, because making up makes it all worth while,' he said ruefully. 'When I asked you to marry me, I wanted all of those things with you.' His voice

hardened. 'Maybe you had better take the time to
think about whether those are the things you want,
too.'

Her already stricken gaze widened. 'Oh,
but——'

'While you're thinking about it, I don't think
there should be any repeats of last night,' he told
her abruptly. 'You have to be sure about this marriage, Christi——'

'I am sure,' she cried, her arms about his waist
as she rested her head against his chest. 'I want to
marry you, Lucas. I want that more than anything
else in the world.'

'I hope so.' His arms moved slowly about her. 'I
really hope so, Christi,' his arms tightened convulsively, 'because I don't think I could survive
another divorce.'

She trembled at the thought of anything so ugly
happening between them, at the bitterness and hate
that was usually all that was left of such a relationship. They had always *liked* each other, surely
that would never change.

'Our marriage will last for ever, Lucas, I
promise.' She held him fiercely.

His mouth twisted wryly. 'I wonder how many
other couples have made the same promise, and a
couple of years later ended up hating each other
across a courtroom? And the fact that I've already
been married once makes it so much worse,' he
frowned. 'I have two children, two children I love
beyond mere words, and they will always be a part
in my life, often have to be put first, before other

considerations, even a second wife. That isn't going to be easy for any woman to live with.' He shook his head self-disgustedly. 'I had no right to involve you in the mess I've made of my life——'

'I *want* to be involved,' she assured him firmly.

He looked down at her with dark eyes. 'I should never have taken advantage of you——'

'I've been waiting four years for you to do so!' she attempted to tease.

He gave a slight smile, but his eyes remained sad. 'That doesn't change the way I took advantage of the fact that emotions were running high yesterday, that I made love to you when I had no right to do so.'

'I gave you that right.' She smoothed away the frown from between his eyes. 'And you did offer to make an honest woman of me afterwards,' she reminded teasingly.

Lucas shook his head. 'I don't believe I'm doing you any favours by marrying you——'

'That's for me to decide,' she said, putting silencing fingertips over his lips. 'You'll just have to accept that I'm all grown up now, Lucas, that I'm a woman who knows what she wants. And I want you. And your children,' she assured him softly. 'You know I love Daisy and Robin.'

He rested his cheek against the top of her head. 'I wonder what I ever did to deserve you,' he sighed shakily.

'Ate all your vegetables as a child?' she teased.

She could feel him smile against her hair. 'No,' he drawled.

'Did well in your exams at school?'

His smile widened. 'Not particularly.'

'Were kind to little old ladies and cooed at babies in their prams?'

'Yes to the first, no to the second,' he derided.

'Well, one out of four isn't bad, is it?' She looked up at him lovingly. 'Lucas, I've been waiting years for you to notice I'm a woman——'

'Oh, I noticed,' he said drily.

'Accept, then,' she corrected dismissively. 'I'm not about to let you go now,' she warned. 'Besides, if you cancel the wedding, I'll go contrary on you and definitely be pregnant!'

The humour faded from his face, a haunted look in his eyes. 'Children of our own are—something I think should wait for a while, Christi,' he said softly.

She could have hit herself for the way she kept saying the wrong thing. Of course he wouldn't want any children between them until he was sure Daisy and Robin felt secure of their place in his life.

She gave him a bright smile. 'Then you had better not cancel the wedding, had you?' she teased.

He looked down at her searchingly, his expression clearing slightly. 'Maybe I'd better not,' he conceded huskily. 'I'm not sure how long I'll be able to resist you,' he admitted ruefully.

Christi frowned at him. 'You really mean it about not making love to me until after we're married?'

He nodded abruptly. 'I don't think we should cloud the issue.'

'But I want you, Lucas,' she protested, knowing she *needed* that closeness between them.

He tapped her lightly on the nose. 'You look like a spoilt little girl when you pout like that,' he murmured indulgently.

'I *was* a spoilt little girl,' she reminded irritably. God, after only one night in his arms, the thought of abstinence made her ache inside!

'You're a spoilt *big* girl, too,' Lucas teased affectionately. 'But the answer is still no, Christi,' he added seriously. 'Let's give ourselves time to adjust to the idea of marrying each other, hmm?'

She didn't want to give them time, she wanted to be in his arms tonight, and every other night. But she could see by Lucas's determined expression that he had made his decision and he wasn't about to change it. 'If you insist,' she muttered, giving in with a definite lack of grace; she couldn't help it, she had no pride left where this man was concerned.

Lucas smiled at her bad humour. 'I insist,' he drawled.

'Well, you don't have to sound so happy about it,' she muttered complainingly, moving out of his arms.

He gave a rueful smile. 'Is that really how I sound?' he mused, shaking his head. 'I want you, Christi, probably more than you want me,' he insisted at her indignant snort. 'I'm not at all happy with letting you sleep alone for the next week, I just feel it's the right thing to do. Which isn't to say that I intend staying away from you completely,' he murmured throatily before his lips claimed hers.

Christi felt as if she had been waiting for this kiss for ever; she put all her love into it, feeling his instant response as she pressed eagerly against him.

Joy lit her heart as she knew he did want her, that he must be aching as badly as she was right now.

She whimpered softly as he slowly caressed her body, his hands trembling slightly, their mouths seeking, searching, learning all there was to know about each other.

Lucas was breathing heavily when he moved away slightly to rest his forehead on hers.

'I can't tempt you?' she encouraged huskily.

His mouth twisted. 'Oh, you can tempt me all too easily,' he admitted ruefully. 'But I'm not going to let you,' he added firmly, putting her away from him. 'Shall we have breakfast together?' he encouraged softly.

She nodded wordlessly, her disappointment reflected in her eyes.

Long after Lucas had gone to his own apartment, Christi sat alone in the lounge, wanting him, *loving* him . . .

CHAPTER EIGHT

'I COULDN'T have chosen better for you myself,' Dizzy murmured appreciatively at her side, her green eyes gleaming with mischief.

Christi dragged her own bedazzled gaze away from Lucas as he stood confidently across the room from them, talking to Zach. Tiny Laura was nestled comfortably in her father's arms, quite content to listen to the rich tones of the two men. 'You didn't, did you?' she said ruefully, knowing Dizzy well enough to realise that if ensuring that she dated Dick, Barry and David hadn't worked to bring herself and Lucas together then Dizzy would have gone right on matchmaking until *something* did!

Her friend turned to hug her. 'I can't tell you how much I've longed for your wedding day,' she glowed.

Her wedding day! She was now Mrs Lucas Kingsley—the second. Ordinarily, it wouldn't have bothered her that Lucas had been married before, but waiting for him to mention custody of Robin and Daisy was starting to fray her nerves.

She knew he had seen the children during the last week, to explain to them that he intended marrying 'Aunty Christi', but he hadn't mentioned to Christi his plans for them at all.

It had been a full and busy week, made all the more so by her work on the advertisements, but somehow they had managed to arrive at today with all the arrangements going smoothly. As Lucas had done most of the organising, they probably dared not do anything else!

Only close relatives had been at the actual service, this lavish reception being given for their other friends at one of London's leading hotels.

'I've longed for it, too.' Christi returned her friend's hug. 'Although I'd almost given up hope of it ever happening,' she admitted softly. Lucas was her husband, *her* husband!

Dizzy grinned. 'Zach was most impressed when Lucas turned up at the castle to ask for your hand in marriage.' Her loving gaze rested indulgently on her handsome husband.

Lucas had kept to his original plan to drive up to the Lake District to talk to Zach personally, spending the night there with Dizzy and Zach, and driving back the next day to assure Christi everything was agreed.

She gave a rueful smile. 'Zach's a pushover for the old traditions.'

Dizzy gave her a coy look from beneath lowered lashes. 'He's a pushover for new ones, too,' she murmured throatily.

It never ceased to amaze her how Dizzy had changed since her marriage to Zach; men certainly hadn't been a part of her life until she had fallen in love with him. Now Dizzy was completely sure of her own femininity, secure in her husband's love.

Christi felt a wistful ache in her chest, wishing she were secure of Lucas's love. But he had still made no mention of the emotion, despite the fact that their goodnights had become longer and longer during the last week, each of them reluctant to go to their lonely beds. She would have forgotten Lucas's decision concerning that in a moment if he would have let her, but Lucas seemed determined to play the gentleman now that their wedding was being planned.

'Uh-oh,' Dizzy said indulgently as Laura began to squirm restlessly in her father's arms, giving out a little choked cry at the same time. 'My daughter feels it's time she had something to eat,' she excused absently, her attention all on the tiny bundle who had brought so much more happiness to her and Zach's lives.

Christi watched enviously as Zach's autocratic face filled with unashamed love as he turned to his wife, handing her the baby, excusing both of them as he accompanied Dizzy to the room where she could nurse Laura.

'You look as if you've lost a pound and found a penny,' David murmured softly at her side.

She turned to him with a bright smile, the smile fading a little as she saw his own pain behind the words. She squeezed his arm emotionally. 'There is another door open out there somewhere, David,' she assured him huskily.

He shook off his despondent mood with effort. 'Hey, this is a wedding, remember?' he teased. 'And all us lucky male guests get to kiss the bride!' He suited his actions to his words, gathering her into his arms to kiss her soundly on the mouth. 'Hm,' he still held her as he looked down at her warmly, '*Lucas* is the lucky man.'

She gave a pained frown, pulling out of David's arms to shoot an uncomfortable glance across the room to where Lucas was now talking to one of his friends. He didn't appear to have noticed the exchange between David and herself, and she turned away gratefully. Having lunch with another man was one thing, letting him kiss her was something else, even at her own wedding!

David was watching her shrewdly. 'Although maybe he still doesn't appreciate that yet,' he said thoughtfully, blue eyes questioning.

Christi gave a bright smile. 'He turned up for the wedding, didn't he?' she teased.

David looked at Lucas with narrowed eyes. 'Someone that looks like him did,' he nodded slowly.

Her cheeks were flushed. 'What do you mean?'

He shrugged. 'I want you to be happy with Lucas, Christi—— '

'I will be,' she assured him quickly.

'I hope so.' He still frowned. 'It doesn't seem too good a start to the marriage when the *first* wife is in attendance, though,' he added drily.

Christi felt her cheeks burn again, but tried to remain composed as she saw Marsha and the children join Lucas across the room. 'Lucas naturally wanted his children at our wedding,' she defended stiffly.

David raised dark brows. 'And Marsha just came along to keep them company?'

She had to admit, to herself at least, that she had been surprised when Marsha had been the one to bring the children, instead of the nanny she had been expecting. But what could she have said or done that would have changed anything? Marsha's presence here was already a fact, she had no choice but to accept it gracefully. And that was what she had done, Lucas at her side when they had greeted the other woman at the start of the reception. His own initial displeasure had turned to impatient acceptance as Marsha greeted them warmly, to all intents and purposes delighted with the remarriage of her ex-husband. How could they possibly object to her behaviour after that?

But Christi had to admit she found the situation more than a little awkward, although she realised there was nothing Lucas could do about it, either, without causing an unnecessary scene. And the children's enthusiastic pleasure in the marriage more than made up for Marsha's presence. She couldn't help but feel grateful for the fact that Marsha hadn't tried to poison the children's minds to the idea of her marrying their father. Considering how the other woman had clung on to Lucas all these years, the likelihood of that happening had been a distinct possibility.

'That's right,' she dismissed lightly, not willing to let David, no matter how good a friend he had become, know just how much of a mar on her wedding day having Marsha there had been.

'Well, at least you'll have the same pleasure in attending her wedding next month,' David derided with satisfaction.

And by that time she and Lucas would have been married for three weeks, her position as his wife more than clear. 'I'm looking forward to it,' she murmured softly.

David chuckled at her determined expression. 'Retribution is sweet, hmm?' he mused appreciatively.

'Lucas is *my* husband, that's all the ammunition I need,' she shrugged dismissively. 'And now, if you'll excuse me, I think I'll join them.'

'Let me accompany you,' David offered politely, taking a firm hold of her elbow. 'With a woman like Marsha, you might have need of back-up troops,' he muttered ruefully.

To an outsider, they must look like a happy family gathering, but Christi was more than aware of the tension in the air as she and David joined the other four.

'Now we have two mummies!' Daisy turned to hug her enthusiastically.

Christi returned the hug, shooting Marsha an uncomfortable glance, turning away again quickly as she saw the other woman's mouth tighten angrily.

'Don't be silly, Daisy,' her brother told her with all the authority his extra year afforded. 'You can only have one mummy.'

Daisy looked rebellious. 'But——'

'I'll be your aunt still, Daisy,' Christi explained gently. 'Just like Uncle Julian will still be just your

uncle when he marries your mummy soon.' The last
was added challengingly, although she didn't dare
risk a glance at Marsha, the person the challenge
had been meant for.

'But if——'

'Hey, you two,' David lightly cut in on Daisy's
puzzled question. 'Have you tried the ice-cream
yet?' he encouraged. 'There's a half a dozen
flavours, so I think it must be in your honour,' he
tempted as two pairs of grey eyes turned to him
curiously.

Daisy looked up at her father. 'Really?'

His expression softened indulgently as Daisy still
lisped slightly from where her front teeth were still
growing back. 'I think I did just happen to mention
there would be a couple of children here today who
love ice-cream,' he smiled.

'Strawberry?' Daisy licked her lips.

'I shouldn't be surprised,' he drawled softly.

'And chocolate?' Robin put in hopefully.

'I believe so.' Lucas lightly caressed his son's
cheek.

'My favourites, too,' David enthused, taking a
child by each hand. 'Have you ever tried them both
together?' he was questioning as he led them away
towards the buffet. 'Stirring them into the same
bowl and——'

'Ugh!' Marsha grimaced delicately as David's
graphic description of the awful sounding con-
coction could no longer be heard.

Christi straightened awkwardly, not quite sure
what to do now, although she was grateful to David

for removing the children from what was, at best, a difficult situation to deal with. From the looks on the children's faces as they scooped up the ice-cream mixture, they hadn't at all minded being diverted!

She jumped a little nervously as Lucas's hand on her waist brought her back against his side, flashing him an apologetic frown as she sensed his puzzlement at her reaction. She wished they could just leave to go on the two-day honeymoon which was all her immediate work schedule would allow, for she desperately wanted to be alone with him. David had been right when he had said she looked as if she had lost a pound and found a penny; she had lost her friendship with Lucas, and at the moment she wasn't sure what she had gained in its place!

'You make a beautiful bride.'

She blinked her surprise at the other woman's comment, looking at her frowningly. 'Thank you,' she accepted warily.

Marsha gave a soft laugh. 'I believe your little bride is suspicious of my motives,' she taunted to Lucas.

Lucas looked warmly at Christi. 'You do make a lovely bride,' he told her huskily.

She felt warm all over, and wished they were on their own, so that Lucas could sweep her up into his arms and make love to her. It was the only time she had felt secure in their relationship.

'Lucas and I were just discussing the plans for when I go away on my honeymoon,' Marsha put in abruptly.

Christi turned to her sharply, the intimacy between Lucas and herself broken. Why on earth should Marsha discuss her honeymoon with Lucas?

'Such a pity the two of you don't have the time for a honeymoon,' Marsha drawled, now that she had their full attention.

'Oh, but——'

'Christi has a contract to fulfil.' Lucas spoke smoothly over Christi's protest.

Marsha nodded. 'It's a pity you didn't have more consideration for *my* career when we were married,' she bit out waspishly.

His mouth tightened. 'I made a lot of mistakes during our marriage that I don't intend to repeat with Christi,' he rasped.

Hazel eyes blazed with anger, the anger fading to a rueful grimace as Marsha saw Christi was watching them with frowning puzzlement. 'Poor Christi doesn't have any idea what we're talking about,' she mused. 'I used to be the fashion editor for a top magazine,' she explained ruefully. 'At the time Lucas didn't approve of his wife working,' she added harshly. 'And, like the fool I was, because I wanted to please him, I gave up my job. The beginning of the end.' She shook her head. 'I was no longer the woman he had married, and I resented him for denying me my career. And having children, believing they will hold the marriage together, is the worst thing you can do,' she sighed. 'All that does is introduce innocents into the mess you've already made of your life.'

Christi had never heard any of this before, had had no idea Marsha had ever had such a demanding career, let alone realised the problems it had caused to the marriage. And what Marsha had just said about Robin and Daisy gave her a whole new insight into their births.

But she had no doubt that, whatever beliefs Lucas used to have about women working and having a career, he no longer felt the same way, for he had always encouraged her career, and he had been the one to insist that their honeymoon should be delayed until after her work was finished on the advertisements.

His arms tightened about her waist as he answered Marsha. 'I told you, I've learnt from my mistakes,' he ground out.

Marsha forced one of her beautiful smiles, shaking off the memories with effort. 'Of course you have,' she dismissed lightly. 'We've both made new starts. Which brings us right back to the arrangements we were making for when Julian and I are away. Having two young children suddenly thrust upon you for a month isn't going to be easy, but——'

'Marsha,' Lucas cut in warningly.

'——Robin and Daisy like you already, Christi, and that's half the battle——'

'Marsha,' Lucas cut in again. 'I haven't had a chance yet to discuss having the children with Christi.' His mouth was a taut line.

Hazel eyes widened. 'You haven't? My God, Lucas,' Marsha said disgustedly. 'I'm sorry,

Christi,' she frowned uncomfortably, 'I felt sure Lucas would have—I wouldn't have—oh, hell!' She glared at Lucas. 'Perhaps you'll let me know when you *have* discussed it with Christi!' She flounced off, crossing the room in search of her two children.

Complete silence enfolded the two of them once Marsha had gone, Christi speechless, Lucas seeming lost in angry thought.

They were to have Robin and Daisy while their mother was away on honeymoon? Lucas was the obvious and natural choice to have the children during that time, although she couldn't help wondering if his motives weren't a little deeper than that. Maybe he would use that month as a trial run for when he applied to have the children with him all the time. She had learnt a new respect for Marsha today, and couldn't help thinking it was an underhand thing to do to take advantage of the situation. But why else would Lucas have waited so long to discuss the children coming to them while Marsha was away, if it weren't because he intended their stay to be a much longer one than that?

Hadn't he realised yet that she would do anything for him, would take half a dozen of his children into their home if it would make him happy?

If this was the way he wanted to do things, she wasn't about to argue. She had known from the first how desperate he was to have Robin and Daisy back with him.

She forced a bright smile. 'I'm sure Robin and Daisy are excited about the prospect of coming to you for a month.'

Lucas sighed. 'I intended waiting until after our honeymoon before mentioning it to you. I felt I owed you that time, at least.' He shook his head irritably.

Two days of happiness before he intended disillusioning her about his real motives for the marriage! She didn't want him to think he 'owed' her anything; the last thing she wanted from him was pity for the decision she had made with her eyes completely open.

'Well, I know now,' she dismissed lightly. 'So we can start making plans for their stay, things we can do, places we can go——'

'All that can wait, Christi,' he told her softly, his eyes gentle. 'We may only have two days, but it is our honeymoon, and I fully intend to make up for the last week of sleeping alone.'

Her heart skipped a beat at the sudden intimacy in his tone, and she looked up at him with widely hopeful eyes. 'We can leave now, if you would like to,' she suggested breathlessly.

'I'd like to.' He gazed around ruefully at their guests. 'But do you think they'll let us go yet?' he derided.

Her mouth quirked. 'I would say they're wondering why we took this long!'

Lucas chuckled softly. 'Then let's get out of here!'

They left amid laughter and good wishes. Marsha, of all people, was the one to catch her bouquet of yellow roses, her pleasure in the act so genuine that, after the initial awkward silence, the good wishes and laughter became even louder.

They had booked into a lovely hotel by the Thames, away from London itself, having decided they didn't want to spend what little time they did have driving to their destination.

Two hours later, having shared a delicious dinner with Lucas in the restaurant downstairs, Christi was glad of the decision. She hurried through her bath, aware of having longed for the moment of being Lucas's wife for as long as she could remember.

Dizzy and Zach had come down a couple of days before the wedding so that Dizzy could help her with the choice of her dress. The white silk dress had been a complete success, Lucas's eyes full of admiration when he'd first gazed at her. But besides the wedding dress Dizzy had insisted that all brides should have 'a nightgown', and Christi had quickly learnt what her friend meant by that. The floaty white creation had narrow ribbon shoulder-straps, lace cups over her pert breasts, satin falling silkily to her feet. It was definitely 'a nightgown', and as Christi gazed at her own starry-eyed reflection in the full-length mirror, she knew that Dizzy had been right to insist that she buy the nightgown; she felt beautiful and desirable, as any new bride should do.

And yet she felt a little nervous about seeing Lucas now. It was one thing to make love with spontaneous abandon, the way it had happened the one and only night they *had* made love, it was something else completely to know that tonight she truly belonged to Lucas, in every sense of the word. It almost felt as if she were married to a stranger, and not her dear familiar Lucas at all.

As she hesitated in the bedroom, the door softly opened, and Lucas watched her from the doorway with caressing eyes. Christi turned slowly to face him, seeing the dark leap of desire in his eyes, and suddenly all her nervousness fled, and there was just Lucas and herself left, her emotions revealed unashamedly as she gazed at the man she loved.

'You are so beautiful, you take my breath away,' he finally murmured gruffly.

He was still wearing the suit he had worn to the wedding, minus the jacket, and he probably wished for a leisurely shower or bath himself; yet, as they gazed at each other, they were both filled with a sudden urgency to be one again, to know each other in a way that would leave no doubts in their minds as to how much they needed each other.

Lucas kissed her long and lingeringly, finally raising his head, his lips only inches from hers. 'Give me a few minutes,' he urged softly. 'Better yet, come and keep me company,' he encouraged huskily.

Christi loved every muscle and sinew of his body, and watched with unabashed pleasure as he stood beneath the shower's spray, muscle and bronzed skin rippling as he soaped his whole body.

And when he finally stepped out of the shower cubicle Christi stood up to meet him, knowing neither of them could wait a moment longer, their gazes locked as they moved slowly into the adjoining bedroom.

It was as beautiful as a ballet, as erotic as a dance, each caress, every movement pure poetry and rhyme as they fitted together in perfect unison, the final crescendo more beautiful than anything Christi had ever imagined before.

As she lay nestled in Lucas's arms throughout the night, awakening to passion often as they constantly sought each other out, Christi knew that she was home, that she would always find her home in this man's arms.

CHAPTER NINE

'BUT when can we come back again?' Daisy demanded petulantly, throwing things into the case that Christi was meticulously trying to pack.

Christi sat down with a sigh, taking the little girl into her arms. 'I don't know, poppet.' She smoothed the silky black hair away from the angrily flushed face. 'You'll have to ask Daddy,' she told Daisy ruefully.

She wanted to do the same thing! The children's month of staying with them was up, for Marsha and Julian would be back from their honeymoon this afternoon, and yet during the last seven weeks of their marriage Lucas hadn't mentioned a thing to her about having the children with them all the time. Surely he had to realise that it would affect her as much as it did him—more so, because she had even less experience of bringing up children than Lucas did, and yet with Lucas out at work all day she was sure to spend more time with them than he did. Not that she minded that; the last month of caring for Daisy and Robin had been very enjoyable. They had enjoyed themselves too, hence Daisy's reluctance to return to her mother. But, if Lucas did intend fighting for custody of them, he was going to have to tell them that himself.

Daisy pouted. 'We could at least have stayed until tomorrow. Mummy and Uncle Julian don't get back until this afternoon.'

'Mummy has missed you so much, she can't wait until tomorrow,' Christi told her reprovingly. 'You know she's telephoned almost every day.' And, considering the newly-weds had honeymooned in the Bahamas, she hated to think what Julian's telephone bill had been like at the end of their stay! But it was unthinkable that he would deny Marsha those conversations with her two children, for he was obviously very much in love with his new bride.

'I wish we could have gone with her,' Robin chimed in from the other side of the room, where he was managing to pack his own suitcase, albeit rather haphazardly. 'She says she's been swimming almost every day,' he added enviously.

Christi knew that Robin's wish bore no reflection on the time he had spent with her and Lucas, it was just that swimming was his passion at the moment, worth any other sacrifice, even that of spending time with his beloved father.

'Now you're being silly,' Daisy told him in a prim voice. 'Children don't go on honey—honeymoon, with their mummy and daddy. Do they, Christi?' she prompted knowledgeably.

She held back her smile with effort. 'Not usually, no,' she admitted.

'That doesn't mean they can't,' Robin challenged his sister, more than a little of the usual sibling rivalry between these two.

It had been a little strange to suddenly find herself a surrogate mother when Daisy and Robin had first come to stay with them. Delicately, she had tried to sort out their squabbles without causing resentment towards her, but, as the days had passed and they had all become more used to each other, she had found she was enjoying caring for the two children, although it was hard work, it was also very rewarding.

Which was perhaps as well, if what she suspected turned out to be true!

Lucas had made it clear from the beginning that he didn't want any more children yet, if ever, and so she had taken the necessary precautions. Unfortunately, something seemed to have gone wrong, and she now had a feeling she had become pregnant as early as their honeymoon—those two nights and days when they hadn't ventured from their hotel room except to eat, and sometimes not even then.

She hadn't dared to even mention the possibility to Lucas, hadn't even gone to her doctor yet to have her suspicion confirmed or denied, longing for it to be true, and yet uncertain of Lucas's reaction to it if she should turn out to be pregnant.

He had so much enjoyed having Daisy and Robin here the last month, and spent as much time with them all as he could. As Christi's work on the advertisements was now over, and the children's school closed for the summer, they had been able to go out for several days.

Christi felt for Lucas now, knew he hadn't felt able to come and help with the packing because he didn't really want to take the children back to Marsha just yet, either. But, until he did something definite about taking the children, none of them had any choice.

She stood up decisively, steadying Daisy in front of her. 'Let's get this packing done so that we can all have lunch,' she suggested, deliberately appealing to the fact that they both loved to eat.

Miraculously, the cases were packed within seconds, and she smiled at the two children indulgently as she went to prepare their lunch. Because she had moved into Lucas's apartment, giving up the lease on her own, and because the apartment only had two bedrooms, she had advised Marsha to give the children's nanny the last month off, preferring to look after them herself for that short time. At least that way, if she made any mistakes—and she had made many!—they didn't have to be witnessed by an expert.

Lucas was already in the kitchen, cooking the hamburgers he had promised the children they could have as their last meal of their stay, turning to smile at Christi as she joined him. The children raced into the dining-room, squabbling over who should be laying the table.

As usual, Christi's heart contracted with love as she gazed at Lucas. Moving easily into his arms, she rested her head against his shoulder. She drew in a quivering breath as his arms tightened about her convulsively. 'We're going to miss them, aren't we?' She spoke sadly.

She could feel him smile against her hair. 'It's certainly going to be a lot quieter around here,' he derided as the argument in the other room became louder.

Once again he had passed up an opportunity she had given him to tell her he wanted the children to come and live with them, and she moved away disappointedly, taking over the cooking of the hamburgers. 'I think you had better go and stop World War Three in there,' she advised dully, her face averted as she sensed him watching her with puzzled eyes.

'Christi?' he prompted softly.

Oh God, why couldn't he talk to her, confide in her? The nights they shared were perfect, couldn't have been more giving, and yet when they were together like this Christi always sensed that Lucas was holding something back from her, that there was a large part of himself he wasn't prepared to give.

'I'm just a little tired,' she dismissed shruggingly, still unable to meet his gaze.

'Taking care of Robin and Daisy has been hard work for you.' He was instantly apologetic. 'How about if we try and sort out some time for our own honeymoon?' He took her in his arms, moulding her body to his.

She made a face. 'I start rehearsals for the new play next week,' she reminded, having finally found work in the theatre again. It was another small part, but an improvement on the last one, where she had only had one line of dialogue!

'So you do.' He released her reluctantly as the sound of breaking glass came from the next room. 'Most of the time, they're very well behaved,' he muttered as he turned to enter the dining-room. 'But when they have a bad day everyone knows about it!'

The smile Christi had shared with him faded as soon as the door closed behind him. She had known being married to a man as complex as Lucas wasn't going to be easy, but waiting for him to confide in her didn't make it any easier. Why couldn't he come right out and say, 'Christi, I want Daisy and Robin to come and live with us'? He had to know she wouldn't say no, that she had never been able to deny him anything. It was the waiting that was upsetting her.

And the fact that she was probably pregnant and feared Lucas's reaction to *that*!

'I think you've actually grown,' Marsha told her son indulgently after hugging him. Daisy cuddled up on her mother's knee, her earlier reluctance to return home completely forgotten in the excitement of seeing her mother again.

Christi and Lucas had driven the children home soon after lunch, finding Marsha and Julian very tanned from their holiday, Marsha more beautiful than ever with her sparkling hazel-coloured eyes and her golden skin.

The newly married couple seemed very relaxed and happy together, and for the children's sake, as much as anything, Christi was glad the relationship so far seemed to have worked out. Although she realised not many marriages failed during the honeymoon!

'We have some gifts for the two of you in the bedroom,' Marsha told the two children affectionately, laughing softly as the children let out excited yells.

'We should be going,' Lucas murmured softly.

Christi was just about to agree when Marsha answered him instead.

'Why don't you and Julian get the children's things from the car?' she suggested lightly. 'Christi and I will go and give this excited pair,' she ruffled two silky heads teasingly, 'their gifts.' And we'll all be civilised about this, her tone seemed to add.

Lucas gave Christi a questioning look, to which she gave a rueful shrug, following the other woman from the room. She stood by while Daisy and Robin admired their gifts, an expensive doll for Daisy, a full American-football outfit for Robin, over which he went into whoops of admiration.

'Julian thought he would like that,' Marsha murmured softly as Robin immediately began to pull the outfit on. She turned to give Christi a rueful smile. 'I don't think I had realised just how much I'd missed a man's opinion about things until this last month.'

Christi gave a tight smile, uncomfortable with the confidence. After all, until a few weeks ago, this woman had seemed to consider her part of the enemy!

'I'm glad you're happy,' she returned stiffly.

Marsha raised mocking brows. 'Are you?' she derided. 'Sorry,' she grimaced apologetically, giving a deep sigh. 'You and I haven't been the best of friends up to now, but I hope that will all change now,' she smiled encouragingly.

Friends? How could the two of them possibly be friends, when Lucas intended using any way he could to take Marsha's children from her?

Over the last few weeks she had come to realise that Daisy and Robin *were* Marsha's children, too. Ever since she had realised *she* could be carrying a child. Even though it was only a possibility she was pregnant, even though she had never held a child of her own, loved it, she knew her heart would break if anyone should ever try to take that child away from her. And she didn't doubt Marsha's love for Daisy and Robin, just as Lucas never had.

She was being torn apart in her loyalties, for she knew that, as the children's father, Lucas had a right to want the children with him, but, as it became more certain with each passing day that she carried a child of her own, she could sympathise with another mother's love for her children, a love that was unique and irreplaceable.

Marsha was so happy at the moment, content in her marriage, reunited with her children. But Lucas was so unhappy, wanting the children to stay with him. What an impossible situation this was!

'I hope so, too,' she answered Marsha with a nod. Although she very much doubted it, not once Lucas had started the battle for the children!

Marsha squeezed her arm reassuringly. 'I really am happy for you and Lucas, you know,' she said softly, Daisy and Robin busy on the floor with their new gifts. 'I know I was a bitch to you before, but—well—I am pleased for you now,' she repeated firmly. 'Julian is absolutely marvellous.' She laughed softly, indulgently. 'Oh, I know he's nowhere near as handsome as Lucas, that everyone probably believes I married him because I fancy myself as a diplomat's wife. You see!' she acknowledged without rancour, as Christi's cheeks blushed guiltily at the echoing of the comment David had made when he'd first told her of Marsha's intended marriage to Julian Holland.

'Julian seems very nice,' Christi told her uncomfortably.

'Oh, he is,' the other woman nodded with certainty. 'But he's so much more than that,' she added lovingly, leaving Christi in no doubt as to her feelings for her new husband. 'He's a man that *needs* me,' she explained with satisfaction.

She gave a gasp. 'Lucas——'

'Never needed me,' Marsha said without rancour. 'Lucas is a man who is sufficient unto himself. Surely you must have realised that by now?' She frowned. 'He's a man who can do anything, be anything he wants to be, and he doesn't need anyone's help or encouragement to do it. My God, he made millions just because he believed he could, and he certainly didn't ask for any help from me.'

'The fact that you were supportive——'

'Didn't mean a damn thing to him,' Marsha dismissed softly. 'He could have gone right ahead and made a success of his life without me. Haven't the last five years proved that?' she derided.

Christi was frowning. 'But you were the one who decided to end the marriage,' she reminded, keeping her voice low so that the children shouldn't hear their conversation.

'Because I was empty inside. Lucas didn't need me, and the love that had been there in the beginning had slowly died through being ignored. All I had left were my children, and I didn't see why they should be caught in the middle of a loveless marriage that was making me bitter and Lucas distant and withdrawn. I did the only thing I could in those circumstances, and put an end to everyone's unhappiness. The children are well adjusted, and Lucas and I were free to find our own happiness as best we could. My only worry over the years,' a shadow darkened the glow of her eyes, 'was that Lucas would one day try to take the children from me.' She shrugged. 'It made me very defensive, but I don't think anyone can appreciate how desolate such a possibility can seem to a mother, how the fear can just eat you up.' She shuddered at the memory. 'Thank God all that's over!'

But it wasn't, it wasn't! Obviously Marsha considered her marriage to Julian secured the children staying with her indefinitely; she didn't seem to have realised that Lucas's own marriage gave him the same advantage. And Christi was no longer sure

Lucas taking the children was the right thing to do. The children *were* well adjusted, for the most part they accepted their lives as they were, and to uproot them now would be to do them more harm than good. In the past, she had thought only of Lucas's happiness, but her own pregnancy changed her whole way of thinking. Marsha's life would be devastated if Lucas should take Daisy and Robin from her, whereas Lucas, for all that he missed the children, had made a separate life for himself.

'Yes,' she agreed dully, forcing a tight smile.

Marsha gave her a searching look. 'Are you feeling all right?' she frowned. 'You look a little pale, and—Christi, are you pregnant?' she said wonderingly.

She raised stricken eyes, swallowing with difficulty. 'I—I——'

'You are,' Marsha murmured softly. 'Lucas must be over the moon . . . You haven't told him yet,' she said self-reprovingly as Christi paled even more. 'Don't worry, I won't say anything to spoil your surprise.' She patted Christi's hand reassuringly. 'You two were made for each other,' she said a little wistfully. 'To us, the children were just what held us together, to you and Lucas they will just be an added bonus.'

If only that were true, but Lucas had already made his feelings more than plain when it came to having more children. He didn't want any at all just yet, if he ever did!

'I'm not quite certain about the pregnancy yet,' she began hesitantly.

Marsha gave her a teasing look. 'What you mean is that you haven't had it confirmed yet,' she mocked lightly. 'Most women are certain before they even get as far as seeing a doctor.'

She *had* been certain for weeks now, had just been putting off the moment it was made official. Because then she would have no choice but to tell Lucas.

'Don't wait too long to tell Lucas,' Marsha laughed softly. 'I can't wait to see his face when he finds out he's to be a father again!' It was said completely without vindictiveness.

There were several other things she had to tell Lucas before she even mentioned the possibility that she might be pregnant and, close as they had become since their marriage, she didn't relish the idea of telling him she no longer believed he should try to take Daisy and Robin away from their mother!

CHAPTER TEN

'WHEN are you going to tell Marsha you intend trying to take the children from her?' Christi asked Lucas steadily, tired of the polite conversation they had been having since leaving the other couple, about how happy they seemed together. It seemed hypocritical when Lucas was poised to shatter that happiness!

She was unprepared for the sudden swerving of the car, accompanied by Lucas's startled exclamation, and was flung forcefully against the door, bruising her side. She watched with wide eyes as Lucas pulled the car over to the side of the road after gesturing his apology to the driver in the car behind for his erratic driving.

An ominous silence filled the car once he had switched off the engine, despite the fact that they were in a built-up area of London. Christi gazed at Lucas apprehensively. The silence became oppressive as Lucas seemed incapable of speech, until finally Christi couldn't stand it any longer.

'Lucas——'

'What on earth are you talking about?' He turned to her fiercely, her own speech seeming to have triggered his own, his eyes glowing silver. 'Christi, answer me, damn it!' he demanded as she hesitated.

She frowned at his anger. 'I know you haven't chosen to discuss it with me yet, but we both know you want Daisy and Robin to come and live with us.'

Lucas became suddenly still, watching her steadily. 'We do?'

'Yes,' Christi confirmed impatiently, turning in her seat. 'You made love to me, married me, so that you could apply for custody of them.'

He drew in a harsh breath. 'I did?'

She sighed heavily. 'Lucas, *talk* to me, don't keep shutting me out!'

His mouth thinned, his nostrils flaring angrily. 'Talk to you? Yes, maybe I should *talk* to you,' he rasped. 'But, you know, right now I'm so angry I don't think I can talk in a rational way that would make sense to either of us! I will say this,' he grated. 'I married you because I love you, have always loved you, even though I told myself for years that I didn't have the right to draw you into the mess I had already made of my life. One other thing,' he pushed his car door open forcefully, 'I never, at any time,' he spoke precisely, cuttingly, 'considered taking Daisy and Robin from their mother.'

'But—where are you going?' She looked at him desperately as he swung out of the car on to the road.

He bent down to look at her, his eyes bleak. 'I'm going to try and walk the bad taste out of my mouth,' he told her harshly.

'But——'

'Drive yourself home, Christi,' he added dully. 'I'm not sure that I've ever really known you.' He shook his head. 'It's certain you've never really known me.' He slammed the car door, walking away.

It took her only seconds to open her own car door and climb out on to the pavement. 'Lucas,' she called to him as he began to disappear among the people milling about on the pavement. 'Lucas!' she cried again as he kept right on walking, the tears starting to fall hotly down her cheeks.

He had gone, disappeared completely among the people who were now starting to gaze at her curiously, obviously wondering what a crying woman was doing standing beside a car parked in a 'No Parking' area.

It was the latter fact that galvanised her into action. Lucas was gone, swallowed up by the crowd; she couldn't just stand here hoping he would come back—especially when she knew he wasn't going to do that! The approaching policeman made her movements all the quicker, for she didn't relish the idea of explaining her predicament to a complete stranger.

How she made the drive back to the apartment she didn't know; she must have been on 'automatic pilot', because when she found herself unlocking the apartment door she couldn't remember any of the drive back there.

Even with the pets milling around for affection, the apartment felt so empty; Lucas's presence was everywhere—and nowhere. This was *his* apartment;

even after weeks of sharing it with him, it still didn't have her mark upon it, and she suddenly felt like an intruder.

Lucas loved her. Had always loved her, he said. She had known the affection was there, but *love*? He had never *told* her he loved her; he had made love to her, then married her, all without the mention of the word love!

Would he ever come back? Would he ever give them a chance to have that 'talk' they so desperately needed to have?

Would she ever have the chance to tell him she was expecting his child?

She had been sitting alone in the apartment for some time, only the steady tick of the clock and the purring of the cats to break the silence, when she heard the key in the door. She sat up with a jolt, startling Gladys off her lap where she had been taking a nap.

She stood up nervously, facing Lucas apprehensively. He looked haggard, his face pale, as if he hadn't managed to rid himself of the 'bad taste' in his mouth.

Then he looked up at her, and there was a light shining in his eyes that Christi had never seen before, and as he opened his arms to her she ran into them gladly, nestling against his chest with a choked sob.

'I hadn't gone far,' he spoke huskily, 'when I realised that I'd never told you how I felt about you, how I've felt since the moment you came crashing into my arms that day so long ago...' His hands cradled each side of her face as he raised it to look at him. 'I love you, Christi,' he said gruffly. 'I've loved you for so long that you've become a part of me I can't live without.'

'I love you, too,' she cried unashamedly, the tears hot on her cheeks. 'I love you so much!'

He nodded jerkily. 'I know, that's why I have the power to hurt you so much. I never wanted to hurt you, Christi, I was just so busy protecting myself, I couldn't do anything else.' He shook his head disgustedly. 'I left myself vulnerable once before, my darling, and I almost had the heart ripped out of me.'

'By Marsha,' she nodded.

'Indirectly.' He frowned, resting his forehead on hers. 'By the time we separated, we both knew it had to be or we would end up hating each other instead of just not loving each other any more,' he explained with a heavy sigh. 'But only one of us could have the children and, although I hated letting them go, I knew Marsha should be the one to take them, that I could stand their loss much better than she ever could. You heard what she said about her career, about how I denied her that,' he reminded huskily. 'Well, it was true. And, because she didn't have her career any more, the children became her whole life. If I had tried to take them away from her, I would have destroyed her completely.'

'But now,' Christi shook her head, 'now she has Julian, and——'

'And I assured her weeks ago, once and for all, that I would never take our children away from her,' he interrupted firmly. 'I doubt that legally I ever could have done, anyway.'

'But——'

'Oh, I'll admit I was devastated by the news that another man was going to have a hand in bringing up my children.' His mouth twisted wryly. 'So devastated that I gave into the weakness of allowing myself to kiss you for the first time.'

The night she had been out to dinner with Dick Crosby! 'I couldn't understand what Marsha was doing there with you that night,' she groaned. 'But I realise now why you looked so grim when you stepped out of the lift.'

Lucas shook his head. 'That had nothing to do with Marsha; she hadn't even told me she intended marrying then.' He gave a rueful smile. 'I was upset at seeing you with Dick Crosby, a man not much younger than me.'

Oh, Dizzy, your plan worked completely! Christi silently congratulated her friend.

'For years I'd told myself I was too old for you, that I had to let you have your own life, your career, friends your own age—and there you were with a man only a few years younger than I am!' he concluded disgustedly. 'By the time you got to Kendrick in the list of three men your friend Dizzy picked out as "suitable" for you, I had decided that if you wanted an "older" man in your life it had to be me!'

'Oh, Lucas!' She looked up at him lovingly.

He shook his head. 'I hadn't meant to kiss you that night you went out with Crosby, but you seemed to be asking me to, and I had held off for so long! Afterwards, I could have kicked myself, I was sure I had ruined the friendship between us.'

She smoothed the anxious frown from between his eyes.

'And I thought you were disgusted by my wanton response,' she murmured ruefully.

'Disgusted!' he snorted. 'I wanted to take you then and there. If you hadn't got out of my apartment when you did, I probably would have done,' he admitted shakily. 'I told myself the best thing to do was forget it, continue as if nothing had happened—and then maybe I could learn to live with the ache that never seemed to leave me! But the night you went out with Barry Robbins I sat in here in a rage of jealousy all night, imagining what the two of you were doing together. I lost control when you actually told me what he did to you!' Even now he was slightly white about the lips.

Christi sighed. 'I was searching for a reaction from you,' she admitted shakily. 'Any reaction!'

'Well, you certainly got one,' he muttered self-derisively.

'And I loved every moment of it,' she told him huskily.

He laughed down at her indulgently, smoothing her cheek with his thumb-tip. 'You're such a baby still,' he murmured regretfully. 'I should never have married you——'

'I would never have married anyone else,' she cut in firmly. 'Oh, I think—even though I didn't at the time!—that you were right to give me those years to grow up, to let me spread my wings, find my own friends, be free to enjoy my career. I'm sure I would be a different type of person if I hadn't had those years to grow,' she acknowledged softly. 'But I've always known who I wanted to spend the rest of my life with.'

Lucas's arms tightened about her. 'I never felt I had the right to you,' he said gruffly. 'Even once I'd asked you to marry me and you had accepted me, I had my doubts, tried to keep my distance, to give you time to back out if you wanted to.'

'I thought you had only asked me to marry you that night because we'd just spent the day with the children and you had realised how much you were going to hate them having a stepfather——'

'Of course I was feeling it that day, and it's going to take me a long time to get used to it. But none of that had anything to do with my asking you to marry me.' He gave a rueful smile. 'Once I began making love to you, that was something I could no longer fight.'

'And children of our own?' she voiced tentatively. 'Is it because you already have Daisy and Robin, because you've been separated from them, that you don't want us to have any of our own?'

'You're only twenty-two, Christi,' Lucas groaned. 'You still have years to give birth in relative safety if you choose to. For now, you have a career that you still haven't conquered as I know you would like to. Children of our own can wait,' he decided firmly.

It wasn't that he didn't want children, he just wanted to give her even more time to just be herself, allow her the freedom he knew had broken up his marriage to Marsha, when he had been so unreasonable in not giving her the same freedom!

Christi stepped slightly back from him, taking hold of his hand to press it gently against her stomach. 'Not this one, I'm afraid,' she told him softly, her face radiant with love when he glanced up at her sharply, only to look down again dazedly to the place where his hand lay.

'When?' he finally managed to breathe.

'I'm not sure, but I think it was the first night of our honeymoon——'

Lucas gave a laugh that was half choked emotion, half indulgent love. 'I meant, when is it due?' he gently corrected. 'But I suppose now I can work that out for myself.' He shook his head in silent bewilderment. 'I'm going to be a father again in just over seven months.'

'If you think Daisy and Robin will be upset because——'

'Daisy and Robin will be delighted,' he assured her drily. 'In fact, they can't understand why we don't already have other children now that we're married,' he said ruefully.

'And you?' She still looked at him anxiously. 'How do you feel about it?'

Lucas looked down at her silently for several minutes, and then a blaze of love unlike anything Christi had ever seen before lit up his face. 'I feel

proud, tender, protective, but most of all I feel love.'
He kissed her gently on the lips.

And that was, after all, all that was important.

'Quick, grab her, before she has the whole lot over!'
Christi warned desperately as her nine-month-old
daughter attempted to reach the branches of the
Christmas tree that lit up the corner of the room.

Robin bent down and gently moved his youngest
sister out of harm's way, getting down on the floor
with her to tickle her tummy. Daisy soon joined in
the game, too.

Lucas chuckled indulgently as he watched the
three children together from across the room, then
glanced up to meet Christi's gaze, love flowing between them like an electric current.

The last sixteen months had been filled with such
love, the birth of Shelley nine months ago only in-
creasing their happiness together. Robin and Daisy
openly adored their new sister, and came to stay
with them all as often as they could. Which was
quite often: Marsha, secure of their custody now,
was able to let them go because she knew they would
always come back. Last Christmas, the two children
had spent the holiday with their mother and Uncle
Julian, but this year Marsha had offered to let them
come to Lucas. In fact, the other couple were
coming to lunch on Christmas Day! Things could
still be a little strained between Lucas and Marsha
at times, but Marsha's happiness with Julian had
enabled her to be more forgiving of the mistakes
she and Lucas had both made in the past.

Lucas crossed the room to join her now, putting his arm about her shoulders. 'Maybe we should have put the tree on a table, out of the way,' he murmured ruefully as Shelley once again crawled towards the illuminated fir tree.

Christi bent to scoop her daughter up out of harm's way. 'Now that she can stand up and move about the furniture, even that isn't guaranteed to keep her out of mischief.' She smiled down at the dark-haired, grey-eyed imp. 'I wish everyone could be as happy as we are, Lucas,' she added with impulsive happiness.

'You're thinking of David, aren't you?' His arms tightened about her shoulders.

The two men had become good friends during the last sixteen months and, like Christi, Lucas felt for the other man's loneliness.

She nodded. 'He said he was going to see his family for Christmas.' She shook her head. 'He's never mentioned them before; I'm not sure he was telling the truth.'

'Wherever he is, I'm sure he's all right,' Lucas assured her softly. 'Now, don't you think we should get these children up to bed?' His voice lightened indulgently. 'Father Christmas is going to be here soon,' he added, just loud enough to throw Robin and Daisy into a frenzy of excitement, their cries of wanting to go to bed completely expected—if virtually unheard of before!

'Father Christmas' carried all three children up to bed, Robin on his father's back, a daughter held in each arm.

Christi followed close behind them. Robin and Daisy might live with their mother most of the time, but they were hers and Lucas's, too. They were a complete family, loving and giving. Most of all, loving.

Harlequin Presents

Coming Next Month

Available in January wherever paperback books are sold, or through Harlequin Reader Service:

In the U.S.
901 Fuhrmann Blvd.
P.O. Box 1397
Buffalo, N.Y. 14240-1397

In Canada
P.O. Box 603
Fort Erie, Ontario
L2A 5X3

Harlequin Romance

Enter the world of Romance...
Harlequin Romance

Delight in the exotic yet innocent love stories of
Harlequin Romance.

Be whisked away to dazzling international capitals...or
quaint European villages.

Experience the joys of falling in love...for the first
time, the best time!

Six new titles every month for your reading enjoyment.
Available wherever paperbacks are sold.

Rom-1

Step into a world of pulsing adventure, gripping emotion and lush sensuality with these evocative love stories penned by today's best-selling authors in the highest romantic tradition. Pursuing their passionate dreams against a backdrop of the past's most colorful and dramatic moments, our vibrant heroines and dashing heroes will make history come alive for you.

Watch for two new Harlequin Historicals each month, available wherever Harlequin books are sold. History was never so much fun—you won't want to miss a single moment!

Harlequin American Romance

Romances that go one step farther...
American Romance

Realistic stories involving people you can relate to and care about.

Compelling relationships between the mature men and women of today's world.

Romances that capture the core of genuine emotions between a man and a woman.

Join us each month for four new titles wherever paperback books are sold.
Enter the world of American Romance.